laptop #6

hot pursuit

Steer Clear of Golden Opportunities

by Christopher P. N. Maselli

Zonder**kidz**

To Lisa and John,
with whom I share many memories
of going to the races

Zonderkidz ®

The children's group of Zondervan

www.zonderkidz.com

Hot Pursuit
Copyright © 2003 by Christopher P. N. Masselli

Requests for information should be addressed to:
Grand Rapids, Michigan 49530

ISBN: 0-310-70665-3

Editor: Gwen Ellis
Interior design: Beth Shagene and Todd Sprague
Art direction: Jody Langley
Printed in the United States of America

03 04 05 06 07 08 /❖DC/ 10 9 8 7 6 5 4 3 2 1

Contents

Contents

Golden Opportunity

Appearances can be deceiving. The inventor whose life was ruined thought he had lost control. Those who ruined his life thought they had control. But neither suspected that the only one who truly held the answer was an unassuming boy in a small American town.

Ka-zapp!

"Zowwwww!"

"Dad?"

"C—close the d—door!"

Matt Calahan slammed the door shut. His dad, sitting on a short ladder inside the entryway, let go of the wrapped wires between his fingers. He licked his fingertips and flicked his hand in the air. "Ow."

"Dad, your hair's sticking up. What are you doing?"

Mr. Calahan frowned and flipped over a piece of paper on his lap. "Installing a security system."

enly jumped to his laptop sit-
ged into the wall. "Um . . . I
w his backpack over by the
down the hallway.
he hurry?" Mr. Calahan asked.
aptop!" Matt shouted. "It's plugged in! A
r surge could fry it!"

Matt's dad dropped his head. "Your dad's getting electrocuted and all you can think about is your laptop?"

Matt stopped at the foot of the stairs. "Well . . . no . . . I just . . ."

Matt knew his dad didn't understand. For Matt's laptop was no *ordinary* laptop. This was the laptop Matt received for his birthday—the one that somehow could "make things happen." Whenever Matt wrote a story in the laptop, it actually happened in real life. All Matt had to do was hit the special key with the clock face on it. Over the past few months, the laptop had become more and more invaluable to Matt . . . and he couldn't imagine losing it. Especially to a silly thing like a power surge.

"Don't worry," his dad said with a smirk. "I unplugged both computers and the TV before I started working."

Matt let out a long breath, walking back toward his dad. "Why didn't you just shut off all the power?"

"I want it on so I can tell when it's working," Mr. Calahan said, as if that made any sense. He looked back at the sheet. "I've been a professional builder for fifteen years. I think I should know how to install one of these newfangled systems."

"You want a comb?"

His dad peered down at him again. "No, but do you see my wire cutters down there?"

Matt glanced at the tools scattered on the linoleum. He shook his head.

"I must have left it at the Zarza's. Since I started remodeling their basement, I think I've left half my tools over there."

Matt looked at the electronic box dangling from the wall. "Is that why you're putting in a security system? Because of the break-in at the Zarza's?"

Matt's dad shoved his tongue in his cheek. "It'll make your mom feel safer."

Just a couple weeks ago, Matt had been shocked when his dad found a bar of gold under some floorboards in the Zarza's basement. The Zarzas were even more shocked. They had no idea when they asked Matt's dad to remodel the dank, underground room that they might become rich because of it.

But what really jolted everyone was when, only about ten days later, someone broke into the Zarza's house. Ironically, nothing was taken ... but the intruder knocked a couple holes in the basement floorboards, presumably searching for more gold.

The break-in, in the middle of their quiet, small-town neighborhood, had everyone on edge. Even Matt's best friends, Lamar and Gill, said their parents were taking extra precautions. "We don't need to be scared," Gill's dad, a security guard, said. "But we need to prepare our houses for the worst. We don't want would-be thieves to suddenly think Oleander Street is an easy target."

Matt's dad grabbed the wires again and carefully twisted them together as if he were French-braiding a little girl's hair. "You know what I want to know?" Mr. Calahan asked his son. "How did word about the gold get out? I know for a fact that Jacinto put the bar in a safety-deposit box for safekeeping until he discovered more about it. Who was there to tell?"

Matt shrugged. "Sometimes," he said, "secrets have a way of getting out."

Pop! The door suddenly opened.

Ka-zapp!

"Zowwwww!" cried Matt's dad.

"Matt?"

"C—close the d—door!"

Lamar Whitmore, from a few doors down, slinked inside and slammed the door shut. His eyes were wide. Matt's dad let go of the wrapped wires between his fingers. He licked his fingertips again and flicked his hand in the air. "Oooow."

"He's installing a security system," Matt explained to Lamar.

"I'm almost done," Mr. Calahan said, his eyebrows furled. Determined, he grabbed the wires again.

"Dad, have you thought about turning off the power?"

Mr. Calahan glared down at Matt. "I'm a professional, Matt, remember? This job doesn't require it. There's not much voltage coming through here."

Matt and Lamar both looked at the hair sticking straight up from Stan Calahan's head.

Matt turned to Lamar. "What's up?"

"Gill and I were just about to go to Alfonzo's and—" Suddenly Lamar's eyes grew big. "Gill! He's right behind—"

Pop! The door suddenly opened.

Ka-zapp!

"Zowwwww!" cried Matt's dad.

"Get out!" Lamar shouted.

Gill, wide-eyed, popped in, popped out, popped back in, shocked Matt's dad again, then shut the door behind himself.

"What's wrong?" red-headed Gill wondered.

Matt's dad patted down his hair. "I'm installing a security system."

Whoop! Whoop! Whoop! Whoop!

The boys covered their ears.

Mr. Calahan shouted, "It's working!"

Matt shouted, "Turn it off!"

Whoop! Whoop! Whoop! Whoop!

Mr. Calahan looked at the dangling control panel, puzzled. "I'm not sure how! The code was . . . let's see . . . 4–2–1–3? No wait. It was 6–2–4–3. No wait . . ."

Whoop! Whoop! Whoop! Whoop!

He pulled the wires apart and the alarm shut off.

Mr. Calahan nodded. "That'll do it."

Gill looked at Matt and Lamar. "With the new baby, my parents have been setting up all kinds of stuff, too," he said. Then, "Hey, Matt, my dad got us tickets to the races!"

"Really?" Matt asked.

Mr. Calahan smiled. "Great! He told me a few days ago that he'd try. It's a police benefit."

Matt's forehead wrinkled.

Gill explained, "There'll be a bunch of cops there watching 'cause they get in free for the next two weeks. It'll be the safest place in Enisburg."

Matt and his dad laughed.

"Cool," Matt said.

"Sorry," Gill said to Lamar, "my dad was only able to get four tickets since he's not on the force anymore. But he's getting more next week so you and Alfonzo can come too."

"Cool!" Lamar cheered. "I might bring Oscar, too, if it's all right."

"You and Oscar getting along then?" Mr. Calahan asked about the man Lamar's mother was dating.

Lamar nodded. "Better. I just don't need to get mixed up with gangster business again." He laughed at his own joke.

"None of you do," Matt's dad said, warning Matt with his eyes.

Suddenly the phone rang. Matt grabbed the cordless off the coffee table. "Hello?" He put his hand over the mouthpiece. "Dad, it's the security company. They said the alarm went off and they need our password."

Mr. Calahan smiled. "Pooka Dookas are supadupa." He glanced at Gill. "You inspired me."

Gill covered his face. Matt gave the phrase to the agent and hung up the phone.

"Let's go over to Alfonzo's," Matt said to his friends.

Gill popped open the door. *Ka-zapp!*

"Zowwwww!" cried Matt's dad.

Gill slammed the door shut. Matt's dad let go of the wires and patted down his hair. He stepped down from the ladder.

"Where you going?" Matt asked him.

"To turn off the power."

Matt, Lamar, and Gill entered the Zarza's house, knocking fists with Alfonzo on the way in. Matt's nose twitched at the spicy smell lingering in the air. He and his friends walked through the entryway and into the adjoining living room. Matt's youth pastor, Mick Ruhlen, was there, sitting on the sofa, talking to Mr. Zarza. Alfonzo's sister, Isabel, sat in a wicker chair across the room. She wore jeans and a red blouse. Her midnight black hair flowed down her back like a waterfall. When Matt entered, their eyes locked for a moment, then she offered a weak smile. Matt returned it.

"Well, I'm just glad everything's all right," Pastor Ruhlen was saying. "I believe God protected you from what could've been much worse."

Jacinto Zarza just nodded.

"He is our hope," Pastor Ruhlen said, pointing up.

Matt and his friends claimed spots around the room. Alfonzo and Gill hit the floor. Lamar sat on the edge of some kind of stool. Matt just leaned against the wall and watched the Zarza's faces.

Matt and his friends had all seen trouble lately— mainly because of his laptop. The boys had quickly discovered that whatever Matt typed into the laptop actually happened . . . and that unknown people "out there" didn't want Matt to have the laptop. But the danger had never quite entered any of their homes.

Now, in the ripple effect of the break-in, Matt could tell the Zarzas felt violated. Alfonzo had turned quiet again, like he was when they first met him. Isabel just looked sad. And their father . . . well, Matt didn't know him well, and he was hard to read. Still, he looked like he had a few months prior when he had first brought his children to the States after a job transfer from Mexico City. Somewhat hopeful, somewhat hopeless. Truth is, Matt always thought the job transfer was just an excuse. The real reason for the move, Matt had discovered, was that Jacinto's wife had left him and left the family in shambles. Matt knew Mr. Zarza and his kids were just looking for a good place to start over.

"We're running in a rat race," Pastor Ruhlen said, throwing a grin at Isabel. "But if we run the race with God on our side, we know that we *will* make it through."

Matt leaned forward and looked back over his shoulder at some photos of Alfonzo and Isabel as children. There were cheesy school photos on blue backgrounds, as well as wonderfully candid shots. From one picture to another, Alfonzo looked like a handful—active and curious. Big, toothy smiles caught the camera. Isabel's deep brown eyes swallowed the lens even as a baby, her black hair shorter, but shiny and straight. Matt turned his head to catch her eyes again. She looked away.

"I guess what I'm saying," Pastor Ruhlen said, his Chia-Pet hairdo blue today, "is: Have you ever made Jesus the Lord of your life?"

Matt blinked.

Mr. Zarza tilted his head. "We go to church," he said. "We have many times."

Pastor Ruhlen nodded. "Yeah, I know you do. I know you really have an interest in getting to know God. That's why I wanted you to know that—dude!— you can make a decision today to put Jesus first in your life. To follow Him above all else. Then when hard times come—like these—you and your family will have Someone you know you can count on."

Matt suddenly felt sick to his stomach. He glanced at Lamar and Gill . . . and then at Alfonzo. Matt, Lamar, and Gill had all been Christians for years. And when Alfonzo—a great guy—moved into their neighborhood, Matt had just assumed he was a Christian, too. He never objected when they prayed. In fact, he joined in. But . . . Matt couldn't say they'd ever talked about whether he served Jesus as his Lord.

Then Matt's eyes clipped to Isabel. *How could I have never asked,* he wondered, *never even thought to ask?*

A sudden rap came at the door and jolted everyone in the room. Alfonzo made his way through the entryway. A brooding man stood in the doorway, with dark, shadowy features and a nose like a hawk. He wore a tattered black coat and equally tattered black slacks. He insisted on talking to the owner of the house. Mr. Zarza excused himself, and Matt and his friends followed him into the entryway.

"Yes?" Mr. Zarza asked the brooding man.

The man's voice was raspy and forceful, not unlike the mobster their friend Oscar had played in the theater. "You have something that belongs to me," he said.

"I don't understand," Mr. Zarza said plainly.

Pastor Ruhlen rounded the corner, behind Matt. Isabel was beside him.

"The *gold bar*," the brooding man bellowed. "I want my gold!"

Matt looked at Alfonzo. Alfonzo looked at Gill. Gill looked at Lamar and whispered, "He's a gangster, isn't he? He's going to put cement on our feet and drop us into the ocean, isn't he?"

Lamar slapped Gill on the chest. "Stop it! We don't need to get into judging people as gangsters again!"

"I don't know what you're talking about," Mr. Zarza told the man.

"Don't play dumb, old man," replied the brooding man. "I know all about it. This used to be my house. I hid my gold in the basement. And I've come to reclaim it!"

Something about this circumstance was oddly familiar. Matt found himself instinctively reaching for his shoulder where his backpack usually sat, so he could pull out his laptop. But it wasn't there. Matt sighed. How he wished he had it with him. He could take care of this situation with a sentence or two.

A deep voice came from the other side of the doorway. "I heard shouting. Is there a problem here?"

The brooding man shifted aside as Mr. Calahan stepped into his personal space. The brooding man opened his mouth to protest, but stopped himself, most likely because Matt's dad looked like a crazy man, his hair sticking straight up on all sides.

"No problem," the brooding man said. "We're just . . . ironing things out."

"Well, if everything's ironed out, then maybe you should be on your way." Mr. Calahan tapped the large pair of wire cutters on his jeans.

The brooding man stiffened his lip and with a haunting growl, he stated, "I'll be back."

He spun around and headed away, swiftly making his way through where the swinging gate used to stand in front of the house.

"*Gracias,*" Mr. Zarza said to Matt's dad, letting out an anxious breath.

"That was awesome!" Matt told his dad.

Mr. Calahan just looked back at the brooding man, a frown on his face.

"I sure wouldn't want to meet that bad dude in a dark alley," Pastor Ruhlen admitted.

"Me neither," Gill said. "I'm glad he left."

Pastor Ruhlen nodded thoughtfully. "Actually, I was referring to Mr. Calahan," he said.

Dodging Danger

2

Dodge ball!"

Matt screamed as the big red rubber sphere spun toward him like a heat-seeking missile. *Pow!* It hit him in the forearm with a blow befitting its launcher, school bully Hulk Hooligan.

Like a tennis-ball machine, Hulk grabbed one ball after another and targeted them at Matt, cracking them against his body as if he were a punching bag . . . which, at this point, he pretty much was.

Matt lurched for any wayward ball he could find, but grabbing one meant exposing an extremity. *Pow! Ooof! Pow!*

"Matt's getting the snot beat out of him!" Lamar cried as he, Gill, and Alfonzo came to Matt's aid, grabbing bouncing red rubber balls and launching them back at Hulk. Even with all three of them joining Matt's side, the two-hundred-and-some-pound beast with bleached blonde hair easily overpowered them.

The only thing that saved the boys from excessive torture was the whistle of Coach Plymouth. "Hit the showers!" he cried.

The four boys let out sighs of relief as the bouncing balls rolled to a stop around their feet. They each grabbed several balls and set them on the nearest rack. Hulk passed Gill on the way into the showers and knocked four balls out of his hands.

Matt stood in the showers and washed up as fast as he could, thinking only about how much he hated showering after P.E. He knew he had to get clean, but he despised feeling awkward and always on the edge of running if Hulk ran through with a wet towel. Fortunately, today he could hear Hulk somewhere in the adjacent room giving someone else a snap-ful of trouble.

Back at the lockers, Matt dried off and put his clothes on as fast as he could. His shirt was sticking to his back so much he had to take it off again and re-wipe his towel across his back. Lamar sat down on the bench next to Matt, then glanced over at Alfonzo, who stood talking to Gill by one of the sinks.

"Hey, Matt," Lamar said, "you think Pastor Ruhlen is right? You think Alfonzo hasn't made Jesus his Lord?"

Matt shrugged. "I don't know—I was wondering the same thing. Kinda weird. He doesn't cuss or anything though."

"No, but that doesn't mean anything. We need to ask him."

"Go for it."

"You're not gonna ask him?"

"I want to . . . but it's more your thing, Lamar."

"My thing?"

"Your thing. You know, asking stuff like that."

"It's *all* our thing," Lamar corrected Matt.

Just then, as if on cue, Alfonzo and Gill walked over and grabbed their clothes from their lockers. As they got dressed, Matt and Lamar exchanged glances. Finally, Lamar just blurted it out.

"Hey, Alfonzo, what did you think about what Pastor Ruhlen said? Have you ever made Jesus your Lord?"

Alfonzo froze for a moment, then looked at Matt and Gill. "I dunno. Never really thought about it."

Matt looked at Lamar. Lamar looked at Matt. Gill seemed oblivious.

"Well," Lamar said, "if you want, we can, you know, pray with you and ask Jesus."

"Ask Him what?"

"To be Lord of your life."

"Oh."

Matt looked at Lamar. Lamar looked at Matt. Lamar obviously wasn't sure how to respond to "Oh."

Just then, Hulk rounded the corner.

"Duck!" Gill shouted.

Hulk guffawed and snapped Gill, Lamar, and Matt with his wet towel. "Gotcha, Calhan!" he prodded.

"Cal-*a*-han," Matt corrected, gritting his teeth.

Hulk continued on his way.

Matt frowned at Alfonzo. "How come he didn't snap you?"

Alfonzo shrugged.

Matt stared at Alfonzo's arms. "Hey— you don't have any bruises either. Didn't he hit you in dodge ball?"

Alfonzo smiled. "Guess it's just my lucky day."

Matt was puzzled. "If I know Hulk, luck had nothing to do with it."

Matt buckled his belt and waited for his friends to finish getting ready.

When Alfonzo pulled his shirt out of his locker, a small square paper hit the ground. Alfonzo bent to pick it up, but Matt beat him to it. Matt flipped the paper over and realized it wasn't paper—it was a Polaroid picture.

"What's this?" Matt asked, looking at the picture. Centered in the picture was the gold bar Matt's dad had found in Alfonzo's basement. It had even been shined up for the picture. Light glared off the bar like the sun's reflection. The only thing *not* shining were some dirty indentations in the top. Matt couldn't believe his eyes.

"Alfonzo, what is this?" he repeated again.

Alfonzo snatched the picture out of Matt's hand and stuffed it back in his shirt pocket. "It's the gold bar," he whispered.

"Why are you carrying around a picture of it?"

"It's cool. Everyone wants to see it."

"But how'd they find out about it in the first place?"

"You know . . . I showed a couple people."

Matt's face dropped. "Did you show Hulk?"

Alfonzo hesitated, then nodded.

"That explains why you don't have any bruises," Gill said gruffly.

"Alfonzo!" Matt nearly shouted. "It's no wonder your house got broken into! You can't parade stuff like this around!"

"No one from school broke into my house," Alfonzo defended.

"But you tell your friends," Lamar put in, "they tell their parents, they tell their friends . . . Word of mouth is a powerful thing."

"Especially in a town this size," Gill affirmed.

Alfonzo pulled the picture out of his pocket. "You think . . . I'm the reason my house got broke into?"

"No biggie," Matt said to his friend. "We all make mistakes. Just . . . get rid of it."

Alfonzo took a step forward. "I'll go throw it away now."

Matt grabbed the picture from Alfonzo's hand. "You don't want it in a trash can here at school." Matt stuffed it into his pocket. "*I'll* take care of it."

"So you guys feel safe enough?" Pastor Ruhlen said, tightening something under the hood of his yellow Volkswagen Beetle.

After school, Matt and Lamar had broken away from the group to go to Pastor Ruhlen's apartment. Lamar had insisted they find out how to lead Alfonzo to Jesus.

"I feel safe," Matt admitted. "I figure, what are the chances of the same bad guy breaking into anyone's house again in the same neighborhood?" *Besides*, Matt thought, *I've always got the laptop.*

"Well, that's swell-er-ino, dude." Pastor Ruhlen's hair, now colored yellow, matched his car. Maybe he got a bulk discount on his hair-care products.

"This is a really cool car," Matt noted. "Is this the V6 model with fuel-injected rotor cuffs and a turbo-pitched drive train?"

Pastor Ruhlen raised an eyebrow. "You don't know a lot about cars, do you, Matt?"

Matt smirked. "Actually I don't know *anything* about them. But I like cars. I think they should have put a backseat in yours."

"Peer inside, dude," Ruhlen encouraged. "There's more room in there than you think. I can be a hip chauffeur if the need ever arises."

Matt peered into the back window. "Wow." There *were* seats back there.

"*Anyway,*" Lamar said, bringing the topic back on track. "So what do we do to lead someone to Jesus?"

Pastor Ruhlen stood up straight and twirled a wrench around in his hand. "My preference is to use the ol' Roman Road."

"What's that?" Matt wondered.

Pastor Ruhlen produced a small Bible out of nowhere. He held it out so Matt and Lamar could see it, then flipped to the book of Romans, chapter 3, verse 23.

"Start here," he said, pointing a finger at the verse. "This Scripture shows that everyone has done stuff wrong—and everyone needs forgiveness." He flipped a few pages over. "Next stop on the road: Romans 5:8. 'But God demonstrates his own love for us in this: While we were still sinners, Christ died for us.' See, the first verse shows we're all sinners.

This one shows Jesus died for us—so we wouldn't have to."

"That's cool," Lamar stated.

"It gets better," Pastor Ruhlen continued, getting fired up. "Next stop, Romans 6:23. It says here that sin leads to death. But if we accept Jesus as our Lord, we will have eternal life. Kinda makes your blood pump, don't it?"

Matt nodded. "But exactly how do we help them make Jesus their Lord? Don't they have to pray?"

Pastor Ruhlen confirmed, "Well, it's really a heart decision for them. But, yes, they need to say something. We're not off the road yet. Next is Romans 10:9 and 10. Go ahead. Read it." He flipped the Bible around and let Matt read.

"'If you confess with your mouth, "Jesus is Lord," and believe in your heart that God raised him from the dead, you will be saved. For it is with your heart that you believe and are jus-tified, and it is with your mouth that you confess and are saved.'" Matt bit his lip. "So all they have to do is say it, and believe it in their heart?"

"Exactly," Pastor Ruhlen confirmed. "Because—verse 13—'Everyone who calls on the name of the Lord will be saved.'"

"That's cool," Lamar said, jotting down the verses.

"That's the Roman Road. Good stuff-er-ino." Then, "So who do you want to lead to Jesus? Alfonzo?"

Lamar nodded. "I'm working on it."

"Sa-weet! You know, sharing your faith is all part of being a 2:52 guy! You know what Luke 2:52 says, don't you?"

At the same time, Matt and Lamar recited, "'And Jesus grew in wisdom and stature, and in favor with God and men.'"

"Right-e-o! Jesus grew smarter, stronger, deeper, and cooler! And when you lead someone to Jesus, not only is it the smart thing to do, but it's deep, dude, because it's what being a Christian is all about!" Pastor Ruhlen stuck his head back under the hood of his car. "Keep me updated, dudes! I'll be prayin' for ya for the perfect opportunity!"

Lying in bed that night, Matt said a prayer for the Zarzas. He prayed that God would give Lamar just the right words when he talked to Alfonzo about Jesus. He prayed that the Zarza's fear would go away and things could get back to normal.

Click!

Matt's eyes popped open. *What was that?*

Pop! Matt sat up in bed. He had definitely heard something. Downstairs. A cold chill crept down his spine. Someone? In his house? *The alarm*, Matt thought. *It's not set.* Matt and his mother were leaving it off until Matt's dad got home from a late evening lumber-shopping trip. Matt pushed his covers aside and cracked open his door.

Pop! There was the sound again. Matt wished he had a dog. He softly closed his door and looked at his desk. Sitting on top was Alfonzo's picture of his gold bar. *Is the burglar back? Looking for more?*

Matt felt frozen for a long moment, not knowing what to do. Gill's dad had warned them about break-ins in the neighborhood. But Matt never truly thought it would happen in *his* house. He held his hand out in front of him. It was shaking.

Matt's eyes darted to the other object on his desk: his laptop. He smirked. His dad wondered why he was always thinking about his laptop. *This* was why. He *needed* the laptop . . . for in situations like this, it could change everything. Matt walked to his desk, tossed the picture of the gold in the trash, and fired up his computer.

This thief isn't getting far, Matt thought. But . . . what if the sounds downstairs were from someone connected *to* the laptop? Matt and his friends worked hard to keep the laptop a secret. They didn't let anyone know about it, not even their parents—it was too dangerous. Matt's dad had picked the computer up at a local pawn shop, and ever since then, Matt had received clues to its mysterious origins. There were people out there who wanted the laptop back. The previous owner—"Sam"—had contacted Matt, warning him to be careful of *them*, whoever *they* were. And now Matt couldn't help but wonder if *they* had found his house.

With the laptop fully booted, Matt opened the word processor. He held out his hand again. It had stopped shaking. He unplugged the computer from the wall and carried it to his door. Quietly, he opened the door and made his way to the stairs. He wanted to see exactly what the intruder was doing, so he could best stop him in his tracks. If there was one thing he'd learned using the laptop, it was to be *specific*. And being specific meant knowing exactly what was happening at all times.

There! A shadow! Matt watched as it made its way across the living room. His heart skipped a beat and his hands felt sticky. Quickly, without thinking, he typed,

> The guy in my house runs into the wall.

Matt hit the clock key. Immediately, the on-screen arrow switched to a golden clock face, ticking forward, fast and furious. Then it stopped. Matt listened.

Boom! Downstairs, the intruder ran into the wall. Matt smirked. He typed,

> The guy in my house trips and falls over the sofa.

Seconds later, *Ka-boom!* "Oof!"

Matt leaned forward. He could see the security panel's glow from the other room. He thought for a moment and then typed,

> As an after-effect of my dad's faulty wiring, the alarm suddenly goes off, dispatching the police. The guy in my house takes off out the door and runs right into the police.

At once, Matt saw a flash in his living room. *Whoop! Whoop! Whoop!* The alarm went off and the shadow ran past the stairs, to the alarm. Matt heard him hitting the keypad. He smirked. Matt's mother ran out of her bedroom, looking disheveled and surprised. Matt slammed his laptop shut.

"What's happening?" she demanded.

"Someone's downstairs."

The phone started ringing. The security company. Suddenly the alarm shut off and the lights downstairs flashed on. The phone stopped ringing.

"Penny! Matt! You all right?"

Matt looked at his mother. His mother looked back at Matt.

"Dad?" Matt called.

Mr. Calahan rushed to the stairs. "Sorry about that," he said, rubbing his knee. "I wasn't trying to wake you. Not sure why the alarm went off."

"Dad, I thought you were a burglar!"

Mr. Calahan grinned. "Nope—just me. But I think I missed the security call. The police are probably on their way."

Matt rubbed his temples. "I can't believe this."

"Sorry," apologized Mr. Calahan.

Matt's mother yawned, waved good night, and went back to bed.

"I'm going to go out and wait for the police," Mr. Calahan said. "They should be here any moment."

"I'm sure you'll run right into them," Matt said, walking down the stairs.

Stan Calahan looked at Matt. "What are you doing with your laptop?"

Matt felt his mouth go dry. His father just stared at him. A long, awkward moment passed between them.

Suddenly, Matt's dad turned toward the door. "You hear that?" He opened it. Matt walked up behind him. A hollow knocking sound echoed in the street.

"It's a good thing the police are coming," his dad said, staring across the street. "It looks like that creep is back. He's pounding on the Zarza's door."

3

Nacho Problem

I demand what's mine!" said the brooding man in a deep, almost haunting voice.

Matt and his dad made their way up the sidewalk, Matt shivering in his T-shirt and shorts.

Hearing their approach, the man turned and shot Stan Calahan the evil eye, then turned back to Mr. Zarza. Both Alfonzo and Isabel stood behind their father.

"This is a copy of the property deed!" The man held up a rolled bundle of paper. "It proves the house is mine."

Mr. Zarza looked for help from Matt's dad, who had now reached the porch.

Matt exchanged an eyebrow bob with Alfonzo. Isabel didn't look as sad as she had earlier. Now her eyes were focused and determined, simply darting a hello to Matt. She wore a thick robe; Alfonzo was in a white T-shirt and shorts.

"Sir, this may have been your house," Mr. Calahan spoke up, "but it's not anymore. It belongs to the Zarzas now."

"Only because the courts thought I'd abandoned it. But obviously, I'm back."

"That will never hold up in court," Matt's dad pointed out.

"There are other ways to get them out of this house."

"Not legally."

The brooding man conceded the point with a smirk, then looked back at Mr. Zarza. "Hand over the gold and we can forget about this whole thing. You don't want this old house to be ... condemned, do you?"

Mr. Zarza narrowed his eyes.

"Look, the police are on their way," Stan Calahan said. "Why don't we let *them* handle this?"

Just then, flashing lights rounded the corner of Oleander Street. The brooding man glanced at them out of the corner of one eye, then threw his papers at Mr. Zarza, who immediately jumped back. Matt's dad lifted his arms and balled his fists, but the brooding man ran down the walk, slid into an old, olive-green Buick LeSabre, and sped off.

Matt's dad suddenly took off down the sidewalk, blank pages flying around him as he ran.

"Where you going?" Matt cried.

"To get his license plate!"

But his dad was too late. Instead, he ran into the police, which didn't surprise Matt at all.

The stock-car races took place on a dirt track about twenty-five miles from the heart of Enisburg. They were a monthly weekend getaway-and-have-fun for the town. Friday night, 6 p.m. was hand-written on many calendars throughout the city. For the next two weekends, however, special tickets were required. It was the "Policemen's Have-a-Ball," a yearly benefit, especially scheduled for police officers, their families, and their friends. Gill's dad was no longer a police officer; he was now a guard at Security Bank. But he still had a lot of friends on the force, making it easy to get tickets to the event.

The crowd was already roaring in the stands, nearly drowning out the roar of the stock cars ripping around the track.

"I didn't know police officers could be this rowdy," Matt yelled to Gill.

"What?" Gill yelled back.

"I said, I didn't think police officers could be this rowdy!"

"I have *what* on my body?"

"Never mind!"

During a break, Matt and Gill begged their dads to let them check out the pits and grab some food. Mr. Calahan and Mr. Gillespie each spotted the boys ten dollars and told them to stick together. Matt and Gill shot down the stands and headed to the pits.

"So what are you gonna do about the freaky guy bugging Alfonzo's family?" Gill asked out of the blue.

Matt stopped in his tracks. "What do you mean, what am *I* gonna do?"

"With your laptop," Gill whispered. "It can fix *anything*."

Matt nodded. "I know ... I just don't know enough about it yet. I guess I don't know what to say."

"You don't know what to say? I thought you were a writer."

Matt started walking again. "That's *why* I'm a writer. I'm much better at typing my thoughts than saying them. That's why I told Lamar *he* has to talk to Alfonzo about becoming a Christian."

Gill's face wrinkled. "Alfonzo's not a Christian?"

"Where have *you* been?"

Gill shrugged. "Who cares? Use the laptop."

Matt stopped in his tracks again. "For what?"

"To make Alfonzo a Christian."

"You can't *force* someone to become a Christian, Gill."

"Your laptop can do anything."

 Matt continued walking. "Not that."

The boys rounded the corner and suddenly bumped into Hulk Hooligan ... literally.

"Get offa me, Calhan!" Hulk ordered, pushing Matt back in an effort to balance his plastic tray of goopy nachos. He reached down to pick up a nacho chip that fell to the ground. He brushed it off and threw it back into the tray.

"What're you doing here?" Matt asked.

"It's a free country," Hulk said.

"It's the Policemen's Have-a-Ball," Gill pointed out. "It's only supposed to be for police officers, their families, and friends."

"So?"

"So ..."

"So I have a lotta police friends. I've ridden in da back o' halfa deir cars."

Matt and Gill nodded, satisfied.

"How much were the nachos?" Matt asked.

"Five bucks for guys like me who're buildin' up deir muscles for wrestlin'. For puny guys like you, I dunno."

Matt rolled his eyes.

Hulk picked out a chip and threw it at Matt. "Think fast! Dodge ball, Calhan!" He guffawed, picked up the chip, and walked off.

"Cal-*a*-han," Matt shouted back at the big lug. Then to Gill, "You'd think after all we've been through, he'd be a little nicer, wouldn't you?"

Gill looked at Matt like he was crazy.

The pits were rather dirty, as expected, and filled with hustling and bustling crews—mostly drivers' families—providing encouragement, working on the cars, and just hanging out. Matt and Gill strolled around for a while before Matt found the car he was looking for: Number 00—a yellow and green rocket on wheels.

"What's with the double-zero?" Gill wondered. "You'd think they could come up with something more creative. Who runs around yelling, 'I'm number zero! I'm number zero!'"

Matt laughed.

"Oh, no," Gill corrected himself. "You're not number zero, you're double-zero!"

"Hey, look!" Matt said, laughing. "There's the driver!"

Thirty feet away, the young driver was yelling at someone, who was shrinking under his shouts.

"This crummy car!" he shouted. "If it gives out on me one more time, I'm going berserk!" He shoved his hand in front of the man's face. "And look at this! The thing burned me!" Then, like a hurricane on the move, he stormed off.

"What's up with him?" Matt said. "I'd be happy to even be *able* to drive a car like that."

Gill shook his head. "I don't think you could reach the pedals."

Matt grabbed Gill's shirt. "C'mon!"

Before heading back, Matt and Gill looked at some other cars, admiring the big engines and fancy advertisements. As they walked, Gill talked about his baby brother. Matt could tell he was really beginning to like his "little buddy," even though he had a few horror stories involving loose diapers.

When the races were about to start again, the boys took a shortcut to the refreshment stand, cutting under a set of bleachers. Halfway through, they heard the electronic voice: *"Hello, boys."*

Sam.

They immediately stopped walking, and Matt about wet his pants. Sam was the one who had owned the laptop before Matt—the one Matt once presumed was dead. But Matt had discovered that Sam wasn't dead. Sam was very much *alive*. And every time the mysterious stranger showed up, it meant another cryptic conversation that about scared the wits out of Matt and his friends. Though, recently, the four boys had come closer to discovering Sam's true identity . . .

Sam stood in a corner, masked by the darkness under the stands. Enough light shone through for Matt to see the signature black trench coat and snakeskin cowboy boots. Something about it all was eerily unnerving.

"Sam?" Matt questioned, though he knew precisely that it was Sam.

"I've been watching you, Matt."

Matt hated it when Sam said that. "So what's new?" he returned.

"I've been watching you, too, Gill."

"Mommy," Gill muttered.

Matt felt strangely perturbed at Sam's continuing *un*-forthrightness. "What do you want?" he demanded.

"I know about the gold."

"It seems *everyone* knows about the gold," Matt noted. "There's a *Prime Time* special on later this week."

"But I know about the man who claims it is his."

Matt's eyebrows arched. "Really? Who is he?"

"No one to mess with."

"Is he connected to the laptop?"

Two little kids ran under the bleachers laughing. They picked up three empty Pepsi cans and continued on their way.

"No," Sam said. *"If he were connected to the laptop, you'd be dead already."* Sam, always the comforter.

"So what's the big deal? He a gangster or something? Lamar will love to hear that."

Sam's head tilted.

Matt's mouth went dry. "He's a *gangster?*"

"I didn't say that."

"You didn't *not* say it!"

"Just be careful."

"Or what? You'll sick CIVD on me?"

Again, Sam's head tilted. The cowboy boots moved back slightly. *"How ... how do you know about CIVD?"*

 "Secrets have a way of getting out," Matt said. Then he came clean. "I saw the sign in your underground lab. The one that said CIVD—and you added the word *deceit* to it."

At once, Sam seemed on edge. *"You ... you've been to my secret lab?"*

"Duh—you were there."

"Yeah!" Gill chimed in, nervously. "Remember— that was the day we blew your house to smithereens!"

Matt cut his eyes to Gill.

"But . . . I didn't know you were . . . in the lab."

"I know a few things," Matt said boldly. "Anyway, I'm going to get some nachos."

Cutting the conversation short, he grabbed Gill's arm and walked off, pulling Gill with him. Sam stood motionless, obviously shocked at the sudden revelations.

Once they were out of sight, Gill stopped Matt. "Matt! Are you crazy! Don't tick off that freaky cowboy! How'd you get so bold?"

Matt didn't know what had gotten into him. Maybe it was because he had seen his dad stand up to the brooding man so boldly. Maybe he was just hungry. Whatever it was, it took everything out of him. He grabbed onto a nearby light pole and let out a long breath. "I think I'm going to faint."

Back home, after a late night with his dad, Gill, and Mr. Gillespie, Matt tried not to let the whole "Sam" meeting spoil his fun memories of the high-speed racing. Number 00 came in fourth overall, which Matt thought was pretty good considering some of the troubles with the car.

Before heading off to bed, Matt took out the trash. He dumped one canister into another around the house, then dumped all of those into the tin can in the garage. He opened the garage door, then waddled the old tin can down the driveway, sending periodic scrapes echoing down the block. When he reached the curb, he set the can upright and looked across the street. To his pleasant surprise, standing at her mailbox, was Alfonzo's sister, Isabel.

Matt tried to suck in his gut and thrust out his chest naturally. Isabel giggled, and Matt realized he must have looked more like an alien with a back problem than a weight lifter. He relaxed.

Isabel smiled and waved, her fingers tumbling one after another. Matt waved back in similar fashion. This meet-and-greet at their curbs had started to become a tradition between both of them. They never talked about meeting, but it was happening regularly. Well, about four times now . . . way too many for it to be a coincidence. Matt always found himself waiting until he knew the Zarzas were home before doing his trash chores. Isabel must have been doing the same, though he dared not ask her.

Oh, yeah, she likes me, Matt thought. He stepped forward, but forgot about the curb. He went down face first.

"Ooof!" Matt cried, putting his hands up to stop a scarring facial accident.

Isabel rushed over, her deep brown eyes wide with surprise.

Matt quickly pushed himself up, dusting off his pants and the pebbles out of his palms. "Didn't hurt!" he announced through gritted teeth.

At once, Isabel burst out in laughter—more free and loud than Matt had ever heard her laugh.

Matt couldn't help himself. He started laughing, too, amazed at his smoothness. After about a minute, Matt's laughter waned. Isabel's didn't.

She thinks I'm an idiot, Matt thought. He just kept smiling as she finally forced herself to stop laughing.

"You're so funny." Her voice sounded like newly spun honey as she reached out to touch his arm.

Suddenly, Matt forgot about the throbbing pain in his hands and knees. "Yeah, I have a real gift for physical comedy," he said dryly.

Isabel giggled. She wore a purple coat, zipped up tight, and blue jeans.

Matt rubbed his hands together, wishing he'd worn his coat. "So . . ." He wasn't sure what to say next. He shoved his hands in his jeans pocket.

Isabel looked at the ground.

"How you doin'?" Matt asked.

Isabel smiled lightly, then her mood suddenly became sober. She looked up. "Good. All right, considering."

"Yeah."

She took a deep breath. "I'm a little worried about our house."

"That guy's just a creep." Matt remembered what Sam had said, but chose not to say anything about it.

"I know it. I just . . . don't want to move."

"Legally, there's nothing that guy can do."

"I don't think he's worried about legalities. Someone needs to stop him from causing us trouble. My dad'll move rather than put up with that. We came here to . . . well, to get away from trouble."

Matt wasn't sure what to say. He agreed that the man needed to be stopped, but what could anyone do? Isabel was right; a man like that wouldn't care about the law. He would just harass the Zarzas all he could until he *forced* them to move. And Matt knew he couldn't let that happen.

Isabel looked at the street again. Her voice softened as she said, "Hey, you know what Pastor Ruhlen was saying to my dad?"

Matt nodded.

"Well, I heard him say that stuff before in youth group. And . . . I've told Jesus I want to serve Him. But it's all new to me."

Matt listened closely.

"I'm worried because . . . I need to stay here, on this street, to find out more about what it means to live like this. I kinda feel like I need people in my life like Lamar and Gill and—" Isabel's eyes lifted, catching Matt's.

Matt swallowed hard. "I feel kinda guilty."

Isabel's forehead wrinkled. She sniffed. "Why?"

"Because you shouldn't have had to hear about all this in youth group. I should have said something a long time ago."

Isabel smiled again. "Hey, don't beat yourself up."

"I'm not, I just ... what about Alfonzo? Has he—"

"I don't know. He hasn't told me."

Matt nodded. "Hey, I'll get you some Christian music."

Isabel winked, shaking away the moment. "I'd like that."

"It's the least I can do."

They were both silent for a long moment. At one point, Isabel looked back at her house, but she didn't turn.

Matt's eyes drifted to Isabel's house, too—the old mansion towering across the street. At one time it was abandoned and nearly condemned. But then Matt got the laptop for his birthday. And he wrote a story about Isabel moving in. And the very next day, she was there. Of course she had no idea he was the reason she ended up on his street.

"I promise, you're not going anywhere," Matt said finally.

Isabel giggled. "I don't need someone to rescue me. I'm just saying—"

"I know you don't need rescuing," Matt admitted. "I'm not trying to be a hero. I'm just trying to be a friend. And as a friend, I'm saying I'll do all I can to make sure you're not going anywhere."

"And how are you going to do that?"

"I'll think of something," Matt promised. Then, "In fact ... you know ... now that I think about it ..." He turned around, tossed the tin lid off the trash can, and tore open the bag inside.

Isabel asked, "Um ... what are you doing?"

"I took it home and I'm sure I threw it in the trash," Matt said.

"Threw what in the trash?"

"And then I emptied the trash," Matt mumbled, digging through the rubbish.

"Matt, that's disgusting," said Isabel, turning up her nose.

"Here!" cried Matt, lifting out Alfonzo's Polaroid of the gold bar.

Isabel looked at the photo. "It's the gold bar."

Matt held it close to his face. He squinted, turning it to make the streetlight reflect off it.

"There! See that?" Matt pointed to the center of the picture.

Isabel grabbed the photo and held it close to her eyes. She pulled it away. "It smells."

"Look," Matt said, pointing again. "See there? See the dirty indentations in the top of the bar?"

Isabel squinted. "I think so."

As she leaned in, her forehead came close to his cheek. He could smell her clean skin.

"I bet you a hundred dollars, that's an insignia," he said, his voice cracking.

Isabel pulled away. "A what?"

"A marking—a clue—that might tell us where the gold came from."

A question mark popped up on Isabel's face.

"I went to Gill's grandmother's last week and she was watching *Matlock*," he explained.

Isabel nodded. "So if we can figure out where the gold came from . . ."

Matt finished her sentence. ". . . then we can prove it doesn't belong to the creepy guy."

Isabel grabbed Matt's arm tightly. "Matt Calahan, you are a genius!"

"It's nothing," Matt said humbly.

"But who could tell us something about the marking?"

Matt twisted his lip. "It would have to be someone who deals with unique items every day. Possibly someone seedy . . . who sees things no one else sees."

Isabel's bottom lip stuck out while she thought about it. She was still holding onto his arm.

Matt's gaze drifted up to his bedroom window. Suddenly, it was as if he could see through the wall, to the laptop sitting on his desk. *The laptop!* He smirked. It had come through for him again.

"You know," Matt said, "there's this pawn shop I heard about that deals in stuff like this. I think my dad said the owner's name was Big Bo . . ."

Being Watched

4

Click! The doors on Ms. Whitmore's taxi cab (as she called it) locked suddenly.

"What's wrong with you boys?" Lamar's mother asked as they shot down the street at a blistering twenty-five miles per hour. "Askin' me to take you out, then when I agree, you have me drivin' down streets where there're bars on every window ... I'm tellin' you, this is the last time I agree to somethin' like this."

"Aw, Ma, it's safe enough," Lamar protested from the seat beside her.

Matt, Gill, and Alfonzo sat in the backseat. Matt's arms circled the backpack on his lap where he always kept his laptop.

"Safe enough ... safe enough," Ms. Whitmore repeated. "Safe enough only because I'm prayin' a whole army o' angels got their hands on their swords for us."

Gill chuckled. "Buff angels with attitudes! 'Cause this time, it's *personal!*"

"Gill, honey, you need to lay off the video games."

They came to a stoplight. The car stopped, but it was going so slow, it was hard to tell the difference.

"How's Oscar doing in his play?" Matt asked.

Oscar was the man Ms. Whitmore was dating— the first boyfriend she'd had since Lamar's father had passed away fourteen years prior.

Ms. Whitmore nodded. "Good, good. That man can act, I'll say that."

"He had me convinced more than once," Matt said flatly.

"Can we change the subject?" Lamar suggested.

The light turned green and Lamar's mom pressed the gas pedal. "Boy, you know you like Oscar," she said.

"I know," Lamar agreed. "But I hate being reminded about how stupid we acted. Sometimes I wish he *had* been a gangster."

Ms. Whitmore shook her head. "Better not speak it 'less you believe it."

Three blocks later, Ms. Whitmore asked Matt for the address again.

"643 Bauer," Matt told her.

"Well, there it is," said Lamar's mom, nodding forward. "Where are we supposed to park?"

Lamar pointed to an open space, but it was in a fire zone. Finally, Ms. Whitmore said, "Look, you boys hop out and I'll just pull in here and wait for you. But stay together and don't take anything from anyone. And don't talk to anyone. And don't touch anything. And don't use the rest room."

"We won't, Ma," Lamar promised.

A moment later, the boys hopped out, Matt slinging his backpack over his shoulder. The pawn shop was actually called "Pawn Shop"—about as *un*creative as you can get, Matt thought. He wondered if it was owned by the same person who opened "Cleaners" and "Donut." It looked remarkably like every other storefront in the neighborhood—worn down and creepy. Even the bricks looked like they were about to crumble. The large front window had bars in front of it, barricading easy after-hours access to the electronics on display.

Matt was the first one inside the door, causing an automatic bell to chime. The stench of cigarette smoke nearly made his eyes water. How had his dad ever found this place? The store was smaller inside than Matt had imagined; just three aisles, peppered with everything from old vacuum cleaners to CDs. Matt saw several products advertised as only available through special TV offers, like the Fabochef Egg Turbine and the ever-popular Ab-Flux Deluxe Series II.

A man at the counter with greasy black hair lifted his eyes from his newspaper and stared at the boys. He was quite possibly the largest man Matt had ever seen in his life. Hulk had nothing on this guy. The man coughed, tapped his cigarette into a cluttered tray, and went back to reading. Matt, Gill, Lamar, and Alfonzo looked around for a couple more minutes. Matt was mustering the courage to ask the man at the counter a few questions when he beat him to it.

"So," the man said in a gruff voice, "you boys gonna buy somethin'? 'Cause if you're thinkin' about liftin' somethin', you can give that up. Got it?"

Matt looked at Lamar. Lamar looked at Gill. Gill looked at Alfonzo. Matt approached the counter. "Do you sell laptops here?" he asked.

The man cleared his throat. "Sometimes. You tellin' me you've saved enough milk money to buy a laptop?"

Matt shook his head. "No, I was just wondering. Have you ever heard of Wordtronix?"

Wordtronix was the brand name of Matt's laptop. He thought it was worth a shot. The man quickly shook his head.

"Where do you get your laptops?" Matt pressed.

The man took a puff on his cigarette. "Is this twenty questions? 'Cause I don't ask no questions when I get 'em in, so I can't tell you nothin' about nothin', so we can stop playing."

Matt twisted his lip and decided to take another approach. "Um . . . I'm looking for . . . Big Bo."

"Is that right?"

"Yeah. Is he here?"

The man took another puff. "You know, kid. I've owned this shop for fourteen years. You're the first person to come in, take a look at me, and think he still hasta find Big Bo."

"So you're Big Bo?"

"You don't let anything slip by ya, do ya, kid?"

Matt nudged Lamar, who pulled a piece of paper out of his pocket. Matt took it, unfolded it, and laid it on the counter. On it, Lamar had reproduced the insignia from the top of the gold bar. It looked like a bubbly letter "B," but the bottom wasn't closed off, and the backbone had a long, curly tail.

Big Bo glanced at the paper.

"We're wondering if you can tell us if you've ever seen this symbol anywhere."

"You mean other than this piece of paper?"

"Yes."

"No."

Matt looked at Big Bo for a moment. The door chime sounded. Matt turned to see who had entered, but didn't see anyone. He looked at the black-and-white monitor behind the desk, but it only showed them standing at the counter. He turned back to Big Bo.

"This is really important," Matt pressed. "Would you please look at it again? I know you get a lot of stuff coming through here. I was just hoping you might recognize it."

Big Bo chuckled and set down his cigarette. "You're a pushy one, kid." He pulled the paper closer to him and picked up a pair of bifocals. Squinting, he stared at the paper for a moment. "Where'd you see this?"

Matt wasn't sure how to answer.

"On money," Alfonzo said.

Matt nodded. The answer was as good as any.

Big Bo turned the paper around and looked at it from another angle. "You buying anything?" he asked.

Matt looked at Alfonzo. Alfonzo looked at Lamar. Lamar looked at Gill. Gill spun around and looked at the row of cassettes behind him. He surveyed it for a moment, pulled out a title, and slapped it on the counter.

Matt raised his eyebrows. *"The Greatest Hits of Sesame Street?"* he asked.

"It's for my baby brother," Gill said.

"You know that thing won't play in a CD player," Lamar told him.

"It's a quarter." Gill slapped a quarter on the counter.

Big Bo rang him up and pocketed the quarter. "Tax is included," he quipped.

The big man looked at Lamar's drawing again.

"So . . . ," Matt prompted.

"I've never seen it nowhere," he replied. "That's the truth."

"But I bought a Sesame Street tape!" Gill complained.

"It's for your baby brother," Big Bo said. "What've you got to complain about?"

Matt rolled his eyes. He slid the paper off the counter and handed it back to Lamar, who pocketed it.

The boys turned to leave.

"Wait," Big Bo said. "Wait a second."

Matt and his friends stopped and turned.

"Look, if this is real important, I think I know someone who can help."

"Yeah?" Matt asked, hopeful.

"Yeah." Big Bo motioned to Lamar to give him the paper back. He then scratched a name down on the back, along with an address. "This guy's a coin dealer. Best I know. Maybe he can help you."

"Thanks," Matt said, grabbing the paper.

"But there's one thing you should know," the owner said.

"What's that?" Matt asked.

At once, a shadow crossed the floor. The boys all jumped. Big Bo's head turned fast.

"There someone there?" the big man shouted.

Suddenly, the security monitor flickered and popped off. Big Bo tightened his face and reached under the counter, grabbing onto something.

"I think we'd better go," Matt said, pushing his friends.

Big Bo ignored them, eyeing the back of the store.

Matt, Lamar, Gill, and Alfonzo rushed out of the store, nearly crashing onto the sidewalk outside. They spied Ms. Whitmore where they'd left her. They ran to the car and piled in like a bunch of clowns cramming into an elevator.

"What's the rush, boys? You find what you're lookin' for?"

Matt pulled his laptop out of his backpack. He wasn't looking for a chase, but he wanted to be ready if one popped up on him.

"No," Lamar said. "We need to go to another place. On Reed Street."

Ms. Whitmore pulled her car out into the street. "Do I look like the New York subway system? Lamar, I have an appointment in a half hour. I don't have time to escort you around town, boy."

"But—"

"And don't even think about taking a cab. If you're going anywhere, find someone we know to chauffeur you."

With his laptop ready to go, Matt quickly typed. Then he looked up. "Can you drop us off at the church?"

"The church? Now that's more like it. Who you gonna meet there?"

Matt looked out the back window, but it didn't look like they were being followed. In fact, it was oddly quiet. Matt turned back to Lamar's mom. "Pastor Ruhlen," he told her.

"But he's a busy man," Ms. Whitmore replied. "He can't just drop everything for you boys."

"It'll be all right," Matt promised. "His afternoon is free."

"How do you know that?" Gill asked.

Matt turned his laptop to show Gill what he had written:

```
Pastor Ruhlen is available to drive us
to the coin dealer this afternoon.
```

"Oh, yeah," Gill quickly covered. "That's right. He's definitely not doing anything now."

High-Speed Chase – Part I

5

ou know what's wacky?" Pastor Ruhlen asked Matt and his friends. "I had a full afternoon of appointments. Then five minutes ago, they all called and canceled. It's pretty good co-inky-dink for you that I'm free."

Sitting beside Pastor Ruhlen, Matt forced a laugh. "Heh-heh. Yeah."

Matt turned around to wink at his friends and saw Gill shifting in his seat, causing Lamar and Alfonzo, who were sitting in the back with him, to moan.

"Have you ever thought about getting a larger car?" Lamar asked Pastor Ruhlen, nudging for space between Gill and Alfonzo. "You know, you're a youth pastor and may be hauling guys like us around a lot."

"Dude!" Pastor Ruhlen exclaimed. "This Bug is the cream o' the crop for me. May be tight, but man, I'm stylin'!"

Matt grinned at his three squashed friends. "Just like peas in a stylin' pod."

Alfonzo playfully slapped Matt upside the head. "How come you get the front?"

Matt lifted his backpack. "I have luggage."

"More like *baggage*," Alfonzo quipped.

Matt glanced into the side-view mirror.

Pastor Ruhlen caught his glance. "Think we're being followed?" he kidded.

"We could be," Matt stated flatly.

"By who?"

"That creepy guy."

Pastor Ruhlen gave Matt a double take, then looked in his rearview mirror. "Seriously, dude?"

Matt nodded.

"Yo, I'm your youth pastor. If things start looking dangerous at all for you dudes, I'm goin' straight to the police."

"We dudes aren't looking for trouble," Matt said. "But sometimes . . ."

". . . it has a way of finding you," Pastor Ruhlen completed. "So I've noticed. I'm just sayin': trouble pops up, we're outta here."

The boys all nodded in agreement.

"So," Pastor Ruhlen said, looking in the rearview mirror. "Alfonzo. How you doin', bud?"

Alfonzo shrugged. "Good."

"You been talkin' to Lamar or Matt about anything in particular?"

"Like what?"

Matt forced himself to stare out the window.

"Oh, I dunno. Football. School. SpongeBob. Making Jesus Lord of your life. Anything."

Subtle, Matt thought. Then Matt kicked himself. Subtle. When it came to his Christianity, Matt hadn't been anything *but* subtle in front of Alfonzo and Isabel. Why couldn't he be more like Lamar, the spiritual one of the bunch? He just didn't have the words to say.

Alfonzo didn't answer and the ride suddenly turned quiet for several blocks.

Pastor Ruhlen pulled off to the side of the road and put the car in park. He studied the address scribbled on the back of the paper Matt held. "Yup, here we are!" he announced.

"Thanks." Matt popped open his door and exited the car. Lamar, Gill, and Alfonzo squeezed out the small door, climbing over Matt's seat. "You coming in?" Matt asked Pastor Ruhlen.

Pastor Mick Ruhlen glanced in the rearview mirror again. "Dudes, I'm gonna keep a lookout. If there's even an inkling of danger—"

"We're outta here," Matt said. "Gotcha. We'll be out ASAP."

"I'll keep the car runnin'. And if you hear me honk, that means trouble."

"Gotcha."

A moment later, Matt, Lamar, Gill, and Alfonzo entered the nondescript shop. It was in a nicer area than "Pawn Shop" had been; the bars on the windows were spaced farther apart.

The floor was clean, though the air was musty, and the room was surrounded with glass case countertops. Each case was filled with coins on display—all colors, sizes, and countries, as far as Matt could tell. A man at the front of the shop leaned on the back of a counter, reading his newspaper intently. He didn't even seem to notice the boys' entrance. He was in his sixties, Matt guessed, with more bald on his head than hair. Silver wisps danced to the flow of the air in the room.

Matt approached the counter. Surprised, the man jumped, and then smiled. He winked and opened his arms.

"Hi," Matt greeted him. "I'm wondering if you can help us. A friend of yours—Big Bo—I'm not sure if that's really his name, but anyway, he referred us to you. We have a question we wanted to ask."

The man smiled and nodded.

Matt looked at him.

The man pointed to his ears and then waved his hands in front of him. He opened his arms again, as if to say, "Which coin would you like to see?"

Matt turned and looked at his friends. "I have a feeling I know what it was that Big Bo wanted to tell us."

"What's that?" Lamar wondered.

"He's deaf."

"Big Bo's deaf?" Gill cried.

"No." Matt nodded his head toward the old man behind him. "*He's* deaf. Anyone have a pen?"

They all checked their pockets, but turned up empty.

Matt motioned to the store owner that he needed a pen. The man looked around, patted his pockets, and shook his head, frowning.

Matt frowned. "How can you not have a pen?"

"Don't get mad!" Gill protested. "He might be able to read your lips!"

"Can you read my lips?" Matt asked the old man.

He smiled, winked, and extended his arms.

"I don't think so," Matt notified Gill.

The man motioned in sign language. Matt blinked. He turned and looked at Lamar.

"Oh, sure, I know sign language!" Lamar said.

"You do?"

"No."

"Oh. This is no time to be sarcastic. This guy could hold the answer we need."

Gill leaned toward Matt and whispered, "Why don't you use the laptop? Write stuff to him and let him type back to you."

"I'm *not* pulling out the laptop," Matt whispered. "No one uses the laptop but me. If we let him touch the keyboard, all he'd have to do is mistype and he could blow something up."

Alfonzo laughed. "Like *that's* gonna happen! When was the last time we blew ... oh ... never mind."

"Charades!" Lamar exclaimed.

"Charades!" Matt repeated.

"Charades!" Alfonzo shouted, turning to Gill.

"Charades!" Gill cheered. "I love charades! I'm the *best* at charades! Have I ever told you about the time I won $200 in a Junior Charades championship?"

"Yes!" Matt, Lamar, and Alfonzo cried.

Gill huffed. "One day you'll appreciate my talents."

"Let's make it today," Alfonzo said, turning Gill around to face the man.

Lamar put the drawing of the insignia on the counter. The man looked at it, then shrugged.

Gill pointed to the insignia. Then he ran around the shop, pointing to each sign. "Sign," he kept saying.

The man nodded.

"I think he understands," Matt said.

Gill nodded. He stepped up to the man, then cupped his hand behind his ear.

"Sounds like . . . ," Lamar started.

Gill folded his arms across his chest. He trembled.

"Sounds like shiver!" Lamar exclaimed.

Gill shook his head.

"Freeze!" shouted Alfonzo.

"Chilly!" Matt added.

Gill dropped his hands and looked at his friends. "Is this so hard? It's *cold.*"

The man behind the counter understood. He pointed to the thermostat, folded his arms across his chest, and shivered.

"Yes!" Gill exclaimed. "Okay, sounds like cold . . . now . . ." He looked around the room. He rubbed his temples.

"Headache!" Alfonzo shouted.

Gill looked at his friend. "I haven't started yet— I'm thinking." Finally, with his finger, he drew a line around his neck. Matt, Lamar, Alfonzo, and the man just stared at him. Gill drew a line around his wrist. He pointed to his earlobes. He thought. He grabbed the air behind him and thrust his hands forward as if he were using a pickax, chopping away at a cave.

"You're a shackled slave," Lamar guessed.

Gill shook his head.

The old man suddenly threw up a hand, pointing in the air. He rushed to one of the side cases and pointed to a collection of gold coins.

"Yes!" Gill exclaimed. *"Gold!"* He touched his nose to let the man know he'd hit it "on the nose."

The man walked back to the piece of paper on the counter. He pointed to it, then to the coin.

"Yes," Gill confirmed. "That symbol was on gold money. But not a coin. A . . ." He formed a box with his hand and then stretched it.

The man pulled back. He reexamined the insignia Lamar had drawn. He scratched his chin. He looked up at the boys. He chewed his bottom lip. The deaf man then popped open his register and sifted through a couple checks. He pulled one out and pointed to it.

The boys looked at each other.

"Does he want us to pay him?" Lamar wondered.

"I'm not buying anything else," Gill stated.

Matt reached into his back pocket and retrieved his wallet. He pulled out a dollar.

The old man shook his head. He pointed to the check again.

"Wait," Matt said. "He doesn't want money. Look where he's pointing."

The boys leaned in. He was pointing to the bank address.

"Security Bank," Gill said. "That's where my dad works!"

Matt pointed to the insignia. "This"—he pointed to the bank name—"is from here?"

The man nodded.

"My dad works there!" Gill exclaimed again.

"We know," Matt said. "Do you think he can get us in to talk to someone who might know about this insignia?"

Gill nodded. "Hey, he's got a lot of friends there. He foiled a bank robbery, remember?"

"Thank you," Matt said to the old man, nodding.

Lamar, Gill, and Alfonzo nodded, too. The man nodded back.

Honk! Honk! The boys spun around. They looked at each other.

"Why again did Pastor Ruhlen say he'd honk for us?" Lamar asked.

Matt remembered clearly. "Trouble."

"What's going on?" Matt asked Pastor Ruhlen as Lamar, Gill, and Alfonzo piled into the backseat. The youth pastor was peering into his side-view mirror.

"Check it out," he said. "A 1972 olive-green Buick LeSabre's passed me three times now. Keeps cruisin' the block. He should put that thing out of its misery."

"That's our creep." Matt slammed his door behind him.

"We're outta here." Pastor Ruhlen hit the gas and took a sharp turn off Reed and onto Ellis Avenue. The boys looked behind them. A split second later, an olive-green LeSabre rounded the corner, screeching its wheels.

"What's he after us for?" Lamar wondered.

Pastor Ruhlen slowed down as he approached the next signal. As soon as it turned yellow, he hit the gas. By the time the Buick LeSabre hit the light, it was red—but he sped right through.

"He's after us," Matt reasoned, "because he knows we're onto something. And we're much easier targets than Mr. Zarza."

"But we can't even give him the gold!" Alfonzo cried.

"He doesn't know that, dude." Pastor Ruhlen took another sharp turn around the block.

"He's still behind us," Gill noted.

"I can't shake him."

Matt glanced at his backpack. Gill caught his eye and nodded.

"I wanna be in the front seat!" Gill whined.

"No way to switch now!" Pastor Ruhlen returned.

"I'll trade with you!" Matt offered, playing along.

"How you gonna do that?" Pastor Ruhlen asked.

Matt threw his backpack in Lamar's lap. He unbuckled and crawled over the seat, crushing his friends in the process.

"Unsafe!" Pastor Ruhlen cried. "Unsafe!"

Gill squeezed over the seat, taking Matt's place, quickly buckling up.

"Now do you see why my mother doesn't like driving us around?" Lamar chided.

"Danger like this," Pastor Ruhlen said. "It's times like this, all right, that it feels good to know Jesus." Pastor Ruhlen smiled big and took another turn. Behind Pastor Ruhlen's seat, Matt pulled out his laptop. He fired it up, his leg bobbing up and down nervously while he waited.

"He's gotta know we see him," Lamar said, glancing out the back window.

"He knows," Pastor Ruhlen agreed. "But he doesn't care. He knows we have to stop sooner or later."

Matt opened his word processor.

"Just type in that we lose him!" Alfonzo whispered to Matt.

Matt shook his head. "No, that's too general," he whispered back. "We have to be specific or it could take too long." He typed,

```
Mr. Creepy, in the olive-green junk-
mobile, gets cut off at the next
intersection.
```

Matt hit the key with the clock face on it. It ticked forward swiftly, turning from gold to white and back.

Pastor Ruhlen sped through the next intersection. *HOOOOOONNNNNNNNNK!* A dump truck approaching from the right plowed into the intersection behind them, slamming on its brakes, causing its back end to bounce twice. Mr. Creepy hit his brakes and came dangerously close to clipping the front end of his car. He spun around once.

"Matt!" Lamar whispered harshly. "You're not trying to kill him!"

"I didn't type that! Well...I...didn't *mean* that!"

"Be careful!"

Pastor Ruhlen took another turn. "I think we lost him," he said.

The boys let out a collective long breath.

Vrrrrooooommm! The boys collectively gasped. Out from a side street, Mr. Creepy's olive-green Buick LeSabre shot onto their tail again.

"Unbelievable!" Alfonzo cried.

"Inconceivable!" Gill added.

Matt quickly typed:

```
A tire on Mr. Creepy's olive-green
junkster blows suddenly. Not blows up—
just blows out.
```

Matt hit the clock key.

Pastor Ruhlen sped around another corner, recircling the block. Mr. Creepy closed in behind them.

Clank-clang! At once, on the road in front of them, a sharp *something* that looked like metal hit the road from a construction site above. Pastor Ruhlen screamed. The boys screamed. Pastor Ruhlen whipped the car left, then right, quickly dodging the foreign object. In the backseat, Matt and his friends felt like shaken, canned sardines.

Behind them, Mr. Creepy wasn't so fortunate. He swerved quickly, but hit the sharp *whatever it was* with his right-side back tire. *Pow!* The tire blew. The hubcap flew off, smashing into a mailbox. The driver zipped back and forth, but regained control of the car. Sparks flew from the back tire. But he was still coming.

"Unbelievable!" Lamar cried.

"Inconceivable!" Ruhlen added, looking back.

"*Aaaaauuuugggggggghhhhhhhh!!!!*" he screamed when he looked forward again.

"*Aaaaauuuugggggggghhhhhhhh!!!!*"   screamed Matt, Gill, Lamar, and Alfonzo.

At once, Pastor Ruhlen's Volkswagen Beetle hit a flight of wide steps and cruised on up, one bumpy step at a time. He hit the brakes and the car finally bumped to a stop on the top of the flight, just before ramming into the building.

For a moment, all were silent. Matt and his friends gulped and slowly let out their breath.

Behind them, Mr. Creepy's olive-green Buick LeSabre slowly drove away, sparks still shooting from the back tire, an irritating grinding sound filling the air.

"Why's he leaving?" Gill asked. "He had us!"

"I think I know why," Pastor Ruhlen offered.

The boys looked at Pastor Ruhlen. He tapped Gill on the shoulder and pointed forward. There, in front of them, painted on the door they almost smashed into, were the words: Enisburg Police Station.

Pastor Ruhlen opened the door.

"Where are you going?" Gill asked.

"To file a report," Pastor Ruhlen said. "That guy needs to get off the streets."

Alfonzo laughed. "You mean like us?"

"You like danger, don't you?"

"I like adventure."

"There's no better adventure than Jesus—is there, Lamar?"

Lamar pulled his fingernails out of the car seat fabric. "No, but driving with you sure comes close."

6

Tale of the Insignia

Later, after being dropped off at the Security Bank headquarters in Enisburg by Pastor Ruhlen, Matt, Gill, Lamar, and Alfonzo were treated like royalty. The whole building had an air of richness about it. White pillars surrounded the entrance. Gold frames set off every picture of past bank presidents—back to the late 1800s. And the purple carpet in the lobby was so plush, Matt imagined it would be more comfortable to sleep on the floor here than it would be to sleep on his own bed at home.

Matt tried to get his right leg to stop shaking as he stood in the opulent waiting area outside of the bank president's office. He figured his friends were nervous too, because Alfonzo was pacing and Gill stayed at his side, telling him jokes that made no sense. When Gill and Alfonzo were out of earshot, Matt asked Lamar what he'd wanted to know all day. "Have you talked to Alfonzo yet?"

Lamar shook his head. "Not yet. I'm praying for just the right time."

"I'm praying that for you, too," Matt admitted.

Lamar nudged Matt with his elbow. "What about you?"

"What about me?"

"Maybe God will set up a time when *you* can tell Alfonzo about the Roman Road."

Matt brushed off that idea. "I don't remember all those Scriptures and I don't know what I'd say."

"Well, check 'em out again and trust God to help you remember them when the time is right."

"Or you."

"Or me. I don't care. I just want Alfonzo to know about living for God."

"Hmmm," was all Matt could think to say.

"Hey!" the bank president burst out when he stepped into the room. "It's a *great* pleasure to meet y'all!"

Matt and Lamar jumped up and Gill and Alfonzo made their way over.

"I'm sorry I only have fifteen minutes," he went on, "but the banking business is a busy business." Then he laughed. "By the look on y'all's faces, I gather you expected someone taller?"

It was true: Bank President Buck Dollar (yes, really) wasn't much taller than Matt or his friends. Five foot seven inches at best. Matt nearly chuckled at the thought of Big Bo in contrast. *Some day*, Matt thought, *I'll have to get these two together and take a picture.*

President Dollar had inherited his Southern drawl, he told them, from his father, a wealthy Texas businessman. Now, Buck Dollar was proud to carry on the family name and the family drawl. (To get the full picture, insert Southern laughter here.)

"I'm awfully proud to give y'all a tour of my fine bank." He put his hand on Gill's shoulder. "Your dad was a brave man, stopping those Baker brothers the way he did. You tell him, whatever he needs, Buck Dollar will deliver."

"Will do," Gill said.

"Do you want anything? Water? Pepsi? Pie?" As soon as he asked the question, his assistant, a thirty-something woman with short black hair, rose from her seat outside his office.

"We're all right," Matt answered for everyone.

The banker nodded to his assistant, who sat back down and resumed her work.

"So let's see . . . if I know youth, you'll want to start by seeing the vault, won't you?"

"Yeah!" Gill exclaimed.

"Actually," Matt interrupted, bursting Gill's bubble, "we were just hoping for a few minutes of your time. We have something we want to ask you about."

The president smiled. "Of course! Anything!" He gestured into his office and pointed to a comfy-looking set of sofas. "Have a seat!"

Matt and his friends entered the office and sat down opposite the president. Matt felt his body sinking into the sofa as if it were eating him alive. He tried to scoot up a little bit so his knees wouldn't be up to his chin.

Matt nudged Lamar, who pulled the now-wrinkled paper out of his pocket. He studied the insignia again—a bubbly letter "B" with a long, curly tail—and then passed it to the banker.

The small man pursed his lips and quickly looked up at the boys. "Where did you boys find this?" he asked. "An old news story?"

Alfonzo looked at Gill. Gill looked at Lamar. Lamar looked at Matt. Matt opened his mouth to speak.

"Oh, I get it," the bank president continued. "Ever since the Baker brothers, you've been fascinated with bank robberies. Y'all are after my own heart. Well, let's just say: You've hit the mother lode."

Lamar leaned into Matt. "Did he just say 'mother lode'?" he whispered.

"Shhhh."

The president sat back and folded his hands across his stomach. "Let's see . . . it had to be 1972? I think that's right. May have been '74. I'll have to look it up. Anyway, this is the Security Bank trademark from that year. That year *only*. In fact, most people don't even know it was *ever* our trademark—because we never used it in public."

He held the paper up. "See—here's the *B*—that's obvious. And the *S* makes up the backbone of the *B*." He traced his finger along the squiggly backbone.

Matt nodded. It wasn't a *B* with a curly tail. It was an *S* and a *B* mashed together.

Alfonzo shook his head. "But why did you stop using the trademark?"

The short man raised a finger. "Because of a man named Dolt Lesniak. He—"

Matt interrupted. "Wait—'Dolt'?"

"I didn't name him," the president interjected. Then, "Dolt Lesniak was a mobster—a gangster— and a very crafty man."

Lamar threw his hands up. "Why does it have to be gangsters?"

"Dolt was the ringleader of a team of thugs. He fixed to steal a shipment of gold bars from an armored car. And he did—he and his thugs walked away with at least thirty gold bars. That's three bars each—enough for each of them to retire comfortably."

"Wow," Matt said. "I guess so." Matt's interest peaked. Finally, an explanation for the gold bar!

"But what Dolt's team of thugs didn't know," the president continued, "was that he stabbed them each in the back."

"How's that?" Lamar wanted to know.

"The best we could figure it, the *reason* he got a whole team together was because he knew if nine *other* guys were out there with stolen gold, there was less heat on him. He played the odds. So while these nine clowns hem-hawed around and got caught one by one, Dolt laid low and made a quiet getaway."

"So he set up the other guys?"

"Yessir—and got away with three gold bars himself."

Matt blinked. *Three gold bars.* Matt's dad had found only *one.* That explained the break-in at Alfonzo's house . . . and the other two holes in the basement. Dolt broke in to retrieve his other two bars before the Zarzas found them. Now he was after the one that got away.

"We hope," the president said, "that one day we'll catch him. See, we stopped having gold produced with that trademark immediately. That way, if he ever tried to get rid of it, we'd be alerted that it was the gold from the great bank robbery of '72. Or '74." He waved his hand in the air. "I really need to look that up."

Gill suddenly shook his hands before him. "Wait, wait. This was thirty years ago. Isn't the time up on the case? You know, because of the statue of lemon nations?"

Buck Dollar burst into laughter. "That's *'statute of limitations'!* Yes, normally after seven years, there's nothing we can do. But once we discovered what Dolt had done, we went right to the courts and got the judge to agree to toll the statute of limitations."

"Toll it?" asked Matt.

"Toll it."

"What does that mean?"

Gill spoke up again. "It means the seven years are on hold until he returns."

Matt, Lamar, and Alfonzo all looked at Gill.

"I watch *Matlock* whenever I go to my gramma's."

"So," Matt surmised, "if this ... Dolt ... shows up again, you just need to know so you can nab him?"

President Buck sighed. "Unfortunately, it's not that easy. This was quite a while back. We have no security photos, no fingerprints, and no confessions from the other robbers. Apparently, Dolt put a heavy thumb on them. As far as I know, they've all refused to talk for fear of their lives."

"So you need evidence," Alfonzo stated.

The president pushed himself off the sofa and threw his arms down. "Bah, but we'll never get it. I'm sure he's living luxuriously in the Bahamas by now. Unless he really is a dolt, he won't come back to Enisburg anytime soon."

Matt and his friends exchanged glances.

"But I bet y'all wish he would, don't you? Bet you'd like to stop a thief like Gill's dad did, huh?"

The boys all laughed nervously.

Matt gulped. "Us?"

Caught Off Guard

7

That Friday night, the boys were at the racetrack with a mission. Gill was able to get tickets for all of them, for which Lamar and Alfonzo were extremely grateful ... even if they might not see much of the action. In the spirit of things, Matt's dad had bought him a race cap with a "00" on it, sold by the crew of Matt's favorite car. Otherwise, they were all dressed relatively nondescript, in warm grays and blacks. After the first few races, the boys were finally able to break away from their fathers—all sitting in the stands—and were now ready to stop ol' Dolt in his tracks. They stood behind one of the concession stands, going over their plans.

"I still don't think this is the best place to get a criminal to confess," Alfonzo complained.

Matt paid no attention to him. He adjusted the small tape recorder under Alfonzo's jacket and stepped back. "I think that's a good length for the sling. How's it look?"

"Fine," Lamar said. "You can't see it at all."

"How's it feel?"

"It itches," Alfonzo said. "Is this absolutely necessary?"

"It works in cartoons," Gill offered.

"Ah, well, okay then."

"I'm telling you," Matt said, "this is the perfect place for a confession. It's filled with cops again tonight."

"Policemen havin' a ball," Lamar interjected.

"They're *off-duty* cops," Alfonzo argued. "I don't think I've seen *one* of them with a gun!"

"We don't have to capture him," Matt said. "All we have to do is get a confession. Then we have evidence—and with evidence, the police can arrest him, which will keep him from harassing you and taking your house."

"Won't it be a bit loud?"

"We just have to get him to talk close enough to the recorder. It'll work. Just don't get near the crowd."

"And getting the confession is my job *why* again?"

"Because it's your house at stake."

"And you're sure he'll show up?"

"I guarantee it," Matt said.

A short while earlier, he had written in his laptop:

> Dolt the creepy guy made it a special
> point of coming to the races outside of
> Enisburg tonight. He found the crumpled
> flyer our handsome hero, Matt Calahan,
> conspicuously left outside of the
> Zarza's household . . . and he was on his
> way, on a hunch.

The laptop would come through for Matt. It always did.

Matt squeezed Alfonzo's jacket together right where the tape recorder sat. He felt the buttons give under his fingers. "Okay, try it," he ordered.

"What do I say?" Alfonzo asked.

Lamar chimed in, "Say 'Everyone who calls on the name of the Lord will be saved.' That's Romans 10:13."

Alfonzo didn't bite. "How about I say this: 'I'd like you to meet my friend Matt Calahan, the guy who has mistaken danger for adventure.'"

Matt pressed the jacket together again, hitting the stop button. "It's not dangerous, so long as all we do is talk."

"Famous last words."

Matt unzipped Alfonzo's jacket and pulled the player out. He rewound the tape and pushed play.

"E-F-G! H-I-J-K! L-M-N-O-Peeeeeeeee!"

"Oops, it's after Big Bird," Matt said.

Gill's mouth dropped. "That's my tape! For my little buddy! I bought it for him! You stole it!"

"It was the only tape we could find," Matt defended himself. "No one uses these things anymore."

Gill narrowed his eyes. "You owe me a quarter."

Matt ruffed up Gill's hair. Gill tried to ruff Matt's up, but just popped off his 00 cap instead. Matt picked it up and stuck it snuggly back on his head. Alfonzo hit play on the tape recorder again and his voice came through loud and clear.

"I'm not sure what I'm going to say," Alfonzo admitted.

Matt smiled. *I know the feeling*, he thought. "Really it's no biggie," he said. "Once we spot Dolt, I'll hide out with the laptop and type you through it." Too easy. Matt remembered what Gill had suggested—that they use the laptop to lead Alfonzo to Jesus. What would happen if he just typed it in? No, it took more than just going through the motions. It took a real heart-commitment—something that couldn't happen through typed words alone. "Anyway," Matt continued, dismissing his thoughts, "how could anything go wrong?" He smiled wide.

Alfonzo moaned.

"Hey! What're ya guys doin' back here?"

The boys all jumped as Hulk Hooligan popped out from around the corner, a nacho platter in his hand. Matt was sure he felt the ground shake as Hulk leaped onto the scene. Hulk guffawed at the prank.

Alfonzo quickly shoved the recorder back under his shirt.

"Hey! What's dat?" Hulk moved forward.

Matt moved between him and Alfonzo. Hulk growled. Matt moved out of the way.

"You know about the gold, right?" Alfonzo said.

Hulk nodded.

"Well, if the thief shows up tonight, we're going to try and get him to confess that he stole it."

"What good does dat do?"

"If he confesses, he gets caught and Isabel gets to stay next door," Matt explained. "Er ... I mean, *Alfonzo* gets to stay next door."

Hulk stood still for a long moment. Then he nodded. "I have ta say. Dat is da stupidest plan I've ever heard in my life."

"We weren't asking for opinions," Matt barked back.

"Ya should be," Hulk said flatly. "'Cause dat's stupid."

"What would you do?" Matt asked.

"Me? Well, I'd get as close ta him as I could." Hulk leaned into Matt. "And den I'd yell, 'Dodge ball!'"

Matt nearly fell over.

Hulk laughed again, throwing a nacho chip at Matt. "Nice hat," he teased. "Number zero. Way da go. Yer number zero."

"No, he's not," Gill defended. "He's double-zero."

"Hulk! What is your point?" Matt cried. "Do you, in all your infinite wisdom and razor-sharp wit, have a better plan?"

"Da point is," Hulk snarled, "when yer plan don't work, you'll come cryin' ta me to pummel him for ya— which is what ya should be doin' in the first place."

"Whatever."

Hulk turned to go, offering a "Have fun, losers" as he walked away.

Matt let out a long breath. "Why me?"

"Maybe he's right," Alfonzo said. "Maybe we should have a better plan. *Isabel* might like that."

"I didn't mean—" Matt took a deep breath. "Guys, all I'm saying is: The day we run to Hulk Hooligan for help is the day I *eat* my hat."

The first thing the boys did was split up—Gill and Lamar at one end of the racetrack and Matt and Alfonzo at the other. They did this because Gill said they always get the bad guys when they split up on *Scooby-Doo*. Matt wasn't sure that was a good enough reason, but he went along with it anyway. The race-track wasn't huge, but there was a lot of ground to cover on foot. And more than anything, Matt wanted to get the recording done quickly so they could save the Zarza's house and get on with their lives.

The agreement was that whoever saw Mr. Creepy first would stay back and get the others' attention.

 Then, with the laptop, Matt would type Alfonzo through a conversation with Dolt, getting Alfonzo out of there safely as soon as they had a confession. To the average Joe with average resources, this may have seemed risky, but to four sharp boys with one amazing laptop, it seemed to plot through rather neatly.

Only fifteen minutes had passed when Alfonzo started questioning whether anything exciting was going to happen at all. And it was only two minutes later when someone literally yanked Matt under the stands. Matt started to yelp, but then realized it wasn't Dolt Lesniak whose hand was crushing his arm. It was—

"Sam?" Matt cried.

The electronic voice greeted Matt, as Sam's grasp loosened. As always, Sam's face was unseen in the darkness, covered by a hood. But the tall stance, black trench coat, and thin snakeskin cowboy boots revealed his identity.

Matt stepped back. "I know what you're going to say. You're going to say we shouldn't go through with whatever we plan to do—because it could draw attention to the laptop. But we have to save the Zarza's house."

Alfonzo watched, speechless, more than likely surprised at the open dialogue Matt was beginning to have with Sam.

"Listen," Sam pressed Matt. *"Forget that. I need to know something."*

Matt shut up.

"You said you were in my lab. When you were there . . . did you take anything with you?"

Matt didn't have to strain to remember that day in the woods when he and his friends had discovered the old cabin with the secret bunker underneath. He remembered crawling down to the lab and finding computer parts strewn about the brushed metal tables inside. He remembered the ominous newspaper clippings tacked on the wall, and the computer underneath. He remembered finding a CD in the computer and, in the rush of the moment, shoving it into his pocket. When the boys arrived home, they found nothing recorded on the CD, just a blurred picture, a mere unfit piece to a much larger puzzle.

"You did find something."

"I didn't say that."

"You didn't have to. Matt, this means we're almost ready. You have everything we need. I thought we lost it, that we were months away from answers ... but you ... you found it."

"But what is it?"

"A map."

"To what?"

"To them."

Matt gulped.

"I'll be bringing you instructions soon. Be ready."

"But ... I'm not sure I want them."

"You must trust me, Matt. I need you now. More than you know."

Suddenly Matt felt put-off. "Look, if you want me to trust you, you have to start being honest with me."

Alfonzo stepped forward a bit hesitantly. "Matt, I'm not sure provoking Sam is the answer."

"I'm not misleading you, Matt."

"Says the one always in the shadows. The one using the electronic voice. And don't think I don't know how you disappeared that night."

Sam was quiet for a moment, then the curiosity came through. *"What night?"*

"The night at the hotel," Matt answered. "The night I ruined Isabel's dress at the banquet. You met me in the rest room, then you left. When I followed you into the hall, you were gone."

Sam stayed quiet.

"I know you didn't just vanish. You went into the women's rest room next door. It was easy for you."

Sam shifted feet.

"Easy," Matt punched, "because *you* are a *chick!*"

Sam stepped back.

"I've even got a picture of you in the crowd at last month's parade."

"Caw! Caw!"

Matt and Alfonzo's heads snapped to the side. The sound was unmistakable. It was Gill doing his sick birdcall. They'd spotted the creepy, brooding man.

Matt felt a brush of air and when he turned to look at Sam, he caught only the flow of her capelike trench coat and a wisp of her long blonde hair in the light.

Matt let out a long breath. "I'm really not looking forward to meeting with her again."

Alfonzo adjusted the tape recorder under his shirt. "You and me both. You think Gill and Lamar are close?"

At once, Lamar and Gill rounded the corner of the bleachers, rushing by like a blur of speed.

"*Ruuuuuuuuuuuuuuuuuuuuuuuuuuuuuuuuuuuunn nnnnn!*" they both cried.

Matt jumped to the side and looked back at his friend's path. The brooding man was headed their way with long, determined strides.

"What do we do?" Alfonzo pressed Matt.

Matt pushed his backpack up on his shoulder. "There's no time to boot up the laptop without being seen."

"Right! So what do we do?"

Matt looked at the man closing in on them.

"I've got an idea," Matt said.

"What?"

"RUN!"

Matt and Alfonzo took off at full speed in the same direction as Lamar and Gill. They came to a parking lot and dove in between the cars. A moment later they heard the brooding man crack his feet against the gravel and stop. The boys waited. Matt motioned to Lamar, who motioned to Gill, who motioned to Alfonzo. The boys split up and quietly, carefully, crouch-walked to different cars.

Matt reached back to pull out his laptop when he saw a shadow pass over the car he was pressed against.

He froze.

The shadow froze.

Matt could hear the man breathing.

"I know you have the gold, Spanish boy!" the brooding man taunted. "I saw you go into the pawn shop! I saw you go into the coin shop! I know you're trying to find out about it! I know you have it! Give me what's mine!"

"We'll never give it to you, Dolthead!"

The cry came from eight cars away. Gill popped up and dropped back down. Dolt ran toward him, passing Matt without knowing it. Matt jumped up and ran the other way. Suddenly, hearing Matt, Dolt stopped and hesitated. Gill popped up, another four cars over. Then Lamar and Alfonzo popped up, both on the other side of the lot. The brooding man chose to head for Alfonzo. Matt ran back into the area outside the track, by the concession stands. He stopped to catch his breath, then quickly pulled his backpack off his shoulder and unzipped it.

"Run, Matt! Run!" Alfonzo screamed as he ran past him. "I'm going to the pits!"

Matt looked up. He didn't see anyone. The races had started, but a few customers still lingered around. They looked up, too, trained to respond to alarm. Matt hesitated for a moment, and then decided to catch up with Alfonzo. If he lost him, that could be even worse news than being unprepared with the laptop. He rezipped the backpack and slung it over his shoulder once more, then ran toward the pit area where he'd seen Alfonzo run.

Matt sped by several crews, then suddenly heard, "Matt! Matt, over here!"

He looked around and then realized the shouts were coming from underneath an RV. Matt hit the ground and slid under next to Alfonzo.

"Is my life going to end tonight?" Alfonzo asked.

"If it were, what would you do?" Matt asked, surprising himself.

"What?"

"I mean about ... er ... you know ... would you go to heaven?"

"What?"

"Er ... well ... I mean ... just think about it." *Smooth*, Matt thought, *real smooth*.

"Well, get out your laptop. I want to get this over with."

Matt nodded. He flipped the backpack off his shoulder and unzipped it. He pulled out the laptop and turned it on.

Snatch! Matt screamed as he felt the hand grab his foot and start pulling. He kicked with all his might, trying to get free. Alfonzo grabbed Matt's laptop with one hand and Matt's arm with his other.

"Let go!" Matt cried.

Alfonzo let go.

"Not you!" Matt shouted at Alfonzo, who grabbed Matt's arm again.

Alfonzo swung his body around and slammed the hand with his foot, too, causing Dolt to cry out and let go. "Hulk had the right idea," he muttered as they scrambled out from under the other side of the RV.

"No, he didn't," Matt said, pushing himself off the ground. "We're going to get this confession." Just as they stood up, the gangster rounded the front of the vehicle and came at them. Matt and Alfonzo took off as fast as they could. They ran through the gravel, kicking up rocks, as they headed toward the only opening: the track.

"We can't go out there!" Alfonzo shouted over the roar of passing stock cars.

Matt looked behind them. The brooding man was still after them, and closing. Matt zigzagged back and Alfonzo followed.

"Where are we going?" Alfonzo asked.

Matt suddenly stopped. There was nowhere else *to* go. In front of them stood a twenty-foot-high wall, channeling pipes into the pit area. Behind them, Dolt closed in. And he wasn't happy.

Seeing that he had the boys trapped, Dolt slowed his stride. He grinned. Matt and Alfonzo gulped.

"What do we do?" Alfonzo whispered.

Matt tightened his fists. "We pray."

Ka-varoooommmm! Pop! Pop!

At once, the pit entrance filled with the smell of burning rubber and smoke. Stock car number 00 rushed in, spitting up dust and gravel—and braked right between the boys and the gangster. Dolt stopped in his tracks. The driver squeezed out of the window of the yellow and green car, shouting for help from his crew. The pit man Matt and Gill had seen before rushed forward.

"Gave out on me again! Gave out!" the driver cried. "I should have had turn three!" He kicked the car and popped the hood. He stormed around to the front and stuck his hands inside the engine area. "Augh!" he cried, snatching his hand back out.

The lanky man ran to his side. "Burned you again?"

The driver just huffed and stormed away, holding his hand.

Dolt Lesniak stood still, trying not to gather attention. Of course, he knew the car would leave soon ... and the boys would be all his. Matt and Alfonzo exchanged glances. Matt quickly flipped open the laptop. He typed:

```
The pit guy finishes working on car 00
quickly. When he leaves, Dolt-filled
with pride and arrogance-confesses his
true intentions. He admits to his
wrongdoing, and brave Alfonzo gets it
all on tape.
```

Matt hit the clock key.

Seconds later, the lanky man slammed the hood and revved the engine. He barely glanced at the boys, and then ran off shouting to the driver, "It's ready to go! Ready to go!"

Matt and Alfonzo stared in the direction he'd gone, but the driver didn't come back. The car just sat there idling. The brooding man started to move forward again.

"What am I going to say?" Alfonzo whispered.

Matt closed the laptop. "I know. We have to improvise," he said out of the side of his mouth. "I can't be typing or he might suspect something."

Alfonzo squeezed the button on the tape recorder under his jacket.

"We know who you are!" Matt shouted at the brooding man, who had stopped on the other side of the car. "You're Dolt Lesniak!"

"A bank robber and a thief!" Alfonzo accused.

The man smirked. "That is my gold," he said.

"What?" Matt shouted. "We can't hear you!"

"I said," the man shouted back, "the gold in your house is mine!"

Matt looked at Alfonzo. Alfonzo looked at Matt.

"How did you get the gold?" Matt shouted.

The man rushed around the front of the car. Matt and Alfonzo rushed around the back. They ended up standing on the opposite side from Dolt again.

"We know you stole the gold, Bo-bo head!" Matt shouted, using a term Hulk's little brother had once taught him.

"The name's Dolt Lesniak, twerp. And that's right. I stole the gold from the fools at Security Bank—back in 1972. But I got away free and clear and there's nothing you can do about it!"

The man rushed around the back of the car. Matt and Alfonzo rushed around the front. They were now back where they started.

"You're wrong!" Matt shouted.

"Yes," Alfonzo shouted. "You're toast! Because they told the statue of lemon nations!"

The man's forehead wrinkled.

"I think that's 'tolled the statute of limitations,'" Matt corrected.

"They can't prove anything," the brooding man snarled.

"They can if they have a taped confession," Matt said with a smile.

Alfonzo unzipped his jacket and lifted up the tape recorder slung around his neck. The brooding man tilted his head. Alfonzo hit rewind, then play.

Big Bird sang, "E-F-G! H-I-J-K! L-M-N-O-Peeeeeeeee!"

"It's after that," Matt whispered.

Alfonzo hit fast forward.

The man on the tape said, *"The name's Dolt Lesniak, twerp. And, that's right. I stole the gold from the fools at Security Bank—back in 1972. But*

I got away free and clear and there's nothing you can do about it!"

Alfonzo hit stop.

The man screamed and slammed the top of the car. Matt and Alfonzo jumped back. But there was still nowhere to run. They were still trapped with a wall behind them.

"Well, then," Dolt Lesniak said in a biting tone, "I guess I'll just have to eliminate all the evidence."

8

High-Speed Chase – Part II

What gangster Dolt Lesniak did next was the last thing Matt or Alfonzo expected. He dove over the hood of the car.

Under normal circumstances, Matt and Alfonzo would have run around the back to get away. But two things happened almost instantaneously that made the circumstances quite *un*normal. First, Lamar and Gill ran into the area screaming their heads off. They were doing so because of the second thing that happened: *Another* stockcar was speeding toward the pit area, coming right at car 00.

So, faced with the choice of surrendering to Dolt or standing there waiting for another car to crush them, what Matt and Alfonzo did was the last thing *Dolt* expected. They dove *into* car 00.

"This is crazy!" Alfonzo protested, squeezing into the passenger's seat behind Matt.

Matt started out on the driver's side, his laptop under his arm. Dolt had landed on his rear end on the other side of the car, and now dove back over the hood to intercept Matt. Alfonzo pulled Matt back in.

"Hit the gas!" Alfonzo cried.

"I can't drive!" Matt screamed.

"Don't let that stop you!"

Dolt slid off the car and jumped up. He reached out to grab Matt.

Matt stretched. "I can't reach the pedal!"

"I can!" Alfonzo shouted just as Dolt's arm came in the window. He slammed on the gas with one foot, while pressing down on the clutch with the other, and shifting.

The car lurched forward, picking up speed fast. Alfonzo shifted again. Dolt jumped out of the way.

"How'd you learn to do that?" Matt cried.

"My grandpa was a farmer!" Alfonzo shouted back. "I learned to drive old trucks on his farm!"

"Cool!"

"Steer!" Alfonzo ordered, slouched down in his seat next to Matt, still pressing on the gas.

Matt shoved his laptop under his rear end to boost him up. *Thank God for the laptop!* He gripped the wheel. On the other side of the pits, Matt spotted Lamar and Gill, their eyes as big as meatballs when they saw Matt and Alfonzo at the wheel. He expected

Dolt to go after Lamar and Gill and relaxed for only a moment—until Dolt shoved the driver of the new car in the pit area to the ground and slid into his car.

Matt whirled the wheel around and aimed for the only escape route: the racetrack. With Alfonzo bearing down on the gas, they shot forward, entering the arena at full speed.

Vrrrooommmmmm! Vrrrooommmmmm!

Two cars swept past Matt and Alfonzo. Matt jerked the wheel to avoid a collision.

"What are you doing?" Alfonzo cried.

"About eighty!"

Matt turned for a split second to look behind him. Dolt was entering the track, avoiding a collision himself.

"He's behind us!" Matt cried.

"Well, don't let him catch up!"

Alfonzo reached over Matt and grabbed the seat belt, putting it around both of them.

Vrrrooommmmmm!

Vrrrooommmmmm!

Two more cars whipped around Matt and Alfonzo. Matt sped past the stands and wondered how long his father would ground him if he knew it was Matt out on the track.

Alfonzo shifted gears again. Matt felt the car pick up speed.

Zzzzzzzittttttttttttttmmmmm!

"What was that?" Alfonzo cried.

"We just passed someone!" Matt yelled. "We're not too bad!"

At once, from behind, Dolt rammed the boys, full force. Matt gripped the wheel as they jerked forward.

Alfonzo didn't let up.

Vrrrooommmmmm!

Zzzzzzzitttttttttttttmmmmm!

"You know what I think?" Alfonzo asked.

"What?"

"I think life with you and that laptop is loco! Half the time, I don't even know if I'll make it through the day *alive*!"

Matt grimaced. "Sorry."

"No—what I'm saying is . . . I think maybe you're right. I don't know if I'll go to heaven! Like Pastor Ruhlen said, I think I need to make Jesus the Lord of my life . . . before it's too late!"

Matt angled around the next curve. He felt his head swimming. And he found himself smiling. "Really?" he said to Alfonzo. Was this the "perfect opportunity" Pastor Ruhlen had talked about?

"Yes, really!"

"You'll have to talk to Lamar when we get off this track!"

Bam! Dolt hit the back of their car again.

"We might not get off this track!" Alfonzo added.

Zzzzzzzitttttttttttttttmmmmm!

Zzzzzzzitttttttttttttttmmmmm!

Matt's mind raced. *Lord, give me the words to say.* When Alfonzo hadn't known what to say earlier, Matt had told him to improvise. Somehow, that just seemed the right thing to do now, too. Just improvise and go for it. "Follow the Roman Road!" he shouted.

"Where's that at?" Alfonzo cried.

All the verses Pastor Ruhlen had shared with Matt and Lamar jumbled in Matt's head. He looked behind him. Dolt was falling back.

"I can't remember all of them—I'll show you later," he said. "But basically, you know we all need Jesus because we've all done wrong things, right?"

"More so since I met you, I think."

"Ha-ha. But, see, God sent Jesus to die in our place even though he knew we would do wrong stuff all the time and wouldn't be able to make it to heaven on our own."

Zzzzzzzitttttttttttttttmmmmm!

Bam! Dolt again. Matt watched as Alfonzo grimaced and pressed down on the pedal again. Matt veered around the next curb, narrowly missing two other race cars.

Zzzzzzzitttttttttttttttmmmmm!

Zzzzzzzitttttttttttttttmmmmm!

"So without Jesus our wrongdoings lead to death," Matt continued. "But *with* Jesus—"

"We go to heaven!" Alfonzo completed Matt's thought. "I got it! But tell me what to do!"

"Right!" Matt cried. "But are you sure you're doing this because you want to and not just because we're on the brink of disaster?"

"I'm sure! I'm sure! Tell me!"

"Well, if you believe that God sent Jesus for you and raised Him from the dead in your place, just say it! God will hear you! Let's pray." Matt closed his eyes.

"Don't close your eyes!" Alfonzo yelled at him.

Matt opened his eyes. "Right! Okay, just say, 'Father God, I'm sorry for all the rotten things I've done.'"

"God," Alfonzo repeated, "I'm sorry for all the rotten things I've done!"

"I believe You sent Jesus to die for me and rise again in my place."

Alfonzo repeated the words.

"So be Lord of my life today and every day."

"So be Lord of my life today and every day," Alfonzo repeated.

"That's it!" Matt cheered.

"I don't feel any different!" Alfonzo shouted back.

Zzzzzzzittttttttttttttttmmmmm!

"You don't have to," Matt told his friend. "It's not about how you feel today. It's about how you live your life—for God!"

"Sweet!"

"Oh no . . . ," Matt whispered.

Alfonzo's eyes grew big. "What?"

"The two cars in front of us are stopping!"

"It's the end of the race!" Alfonzo screamed.

Immediately, Alfonzo shifted both feet over to the brake pedal. The car screeched to a halt on the track, spinning around as it crossed the finish line.

"Aaaaaaaaaaaaaaaaaaaughhhhhhhhhhhhhh!" the boys screamed in unison.

The car skidded to a stop, slamming into the side of the car in front of them. Matt and Alfonzo glanced back at the track and saw Dolt making his way in, more controlled than they were.

Matt undid the seat belt and the boys caught their breath, their ears ringing.

"Let's get out of this car!" Matt shoved his laptop under his arm.

Alfonzo didn't need any encouragement. He pushed out the passenger side as Matt pushed out the driver's side. When their feet hit the ground, they heard the crowd cheering. Matt and Alfonzo looked up at the stands. All the spectators were on their feet, clapping.

Matt's eyes drew over to the drivers of the cars in front of them. The first one was accepting a golden trophy, speaking into a microphone. The second was having his picture taken with a girl.

Matt blinked and grabbed Alfonzo's arm. "How fast were we going?" he asked.

Alfonzo shrugged. "I'm not sure, why?"

"I think we placed."

Alfonzo gave Matt a push. "Get out of town."

"No, really—I think—"

Suddenly an attractive young woman with long black hair approached the boys and stood between them. She smiled big. Matt and Alfonzo could only stare at her, aghast at what was happening.

Pop! A flash of light hit them in the eyes.

"Congrats, boys," the woman said. "I dunno where Robby is, but you just earned him third place." She kissed each of them, leaving a bright red lipstick mark on their cheeks. The boys wiped their faces in disgust.

"Hey!"

Matt and Alfonzo turned around. Dolt may not have won the race, but he clearly hadn't given up. Anger and frustration contorted his face . . . and he was heading straight toward them.

9

Dodge Ball

Dolt picked up his pace, making a beeline for Matt and Alfonzo. Alfonzo unzipped his jacket and yanked the tape recorder off his neck. The sling snapped like thread.

"Take it!" he said to Matt. "You can get a head start. Save my house."

"I'm not going without you."

"If you stay, he'll get both of us—and my house."

Matt hesitated, looking at the cheering crowd, the rambunctious winner's circle. Then, with determination, he snatched the recorder from Alfonzo with one hand and handed him his laptop with the other.

"Don't let him get this—no matter what," Matt shouted to his friend.

Alfonzo accepted the laptop, cracking it open. Frowning, Matt studied the recorder and hit rewind.

Then he ran straight over to the announcer and grabbed the microphone. "Now hear this!" he shouted into the microphone.

He watched as Dolt stopped in front of Alfonzo, and then froze. He stared ahead at Matt.

The cheering crowd quieted down and Matt pressed the small recorder against the microphone. He pushed play.

Big Bird sang, "E-F-G! H-I-J-K! L-M-N-O-Peeeeeeeee!"

"Sorry," Matt said. "It's after that." He hit fast forward.

A moment later, loudly, into the microphone, a voice emerged. "*The name's Dolt Lesniak, twerp. And that's right. I stole the gold from the fools at Security Bank—back in 1972. But I got away free and clear and there's nothing you can do about it!*"

Matt hit stop.

Dolt stared at Matt.

"This tape was made just a few minutes ago," Matt continued and swung his arm in the direction of the brooding man. "By *that* man," he added.

Matt scanned the crowd, waiting for any off-duty police officers to rush Dolt. Here and there he could see them—reaching for their guns—and all hitting air. There wasn't a gun in the crowd.

Matt gulped. Alfonzo gulped. Dolt grinned. A few officers ran into the aisles, making their way down. But Matt knew they wouldn't be fast enough. This criminal was named Dolt, but he wasn't a blockhead. He turned this way and that, obviously looking for a quick escape.

Frustration began to build up inside of Matt. How could he possibly let the criminal get away now?

Quickly, Dolt started to move. Alfonzo appeared in front of Matt then, the laptop open and booted. Matt didn't have time to think about what to write, he just *had* to write *something*. As fast as he could, he typed the first thing that came to mind:

```
Hulk gets to play dodge ball.
```

He hit the clock key.

"Dodge ball!" a faint voice in the crowd shouted just as Dolt began to bolt.

Dolt froze. With question marks above their heads, the off-duty officers looked for the voice that was shouting insanely.

"Dodge ball!" Hulk Hooligan shouted again.

Dolt shook his head. He started to move again.

Suddenly a nacho struck him in the face.

Then another.

Then a chili dog.

Then a sloppy burrito.

Then a large Pepsi.

At once, a whole barrage of expensive, fast, and flavorful food was pitched over the fence, through the fence, and from all around the area, focused on one target: Dolt Lesniak.

Knocked back by the sudden onrush of junk-food fare, Dolt crouched down and put his hands over his face.

Within seconds, off-duty officers, two men and a woman, had the criminal pinned to the ground, squirming in the mess of dirt and nacho surprise that would have him smelling like the greasy floor of the concession stand for weeks.

"We did it," Matt said, as surprised as anyone.

Lamar and Gill rushed into the winner's circle and gave Matt and Alfonzo highfives.

"You did it!" they exclaimed.

"You guys got to drive?" Gill shouted, clearly more excited about that than apprehending the criminal.

"Yeah—we saved our house *and* we won the race!" Alfonzo said.

"We won more than one race," Matt said, smiling at his friend.

Lamar's mouth dropped. "You mean—"

Alfonzo smiled.

Lamar shouted and gave him a highfive. "And Hulk," he said. "Can you believe that? He actually helped!"

"Well, the *laptop* helped," Matt admitted. "But still . . . Hulk was pretty amazing." And then, to keep his end of the bargain, he took off his hat and stuffed it in his mouth.

Despite the fact that Matt and Alfonzo had helped capture a gangster-at-large, neither of their fathers were pleased that they had put themselves in peril not only with a dangerous man but also behind the wheel of a race car. Matt assured his father that he had worn his seat belt, but it didn't help his case.

"Ace," Mr. Calahan said, "you're grounded."

"But—"

"But *nothing*," his father said. "Ever since . . . I don't know. You know what I keep coming back to? Ever since you got that laptop, you've been getting in *way* over your head."

"That just comes with being thirteen," Matt countered.

"When I was thirteen, I was *never* present at a bank robbery. I *never*—not even *once*—got lost in the wilderness. I *never* accused an actor of being a gangster in front of my hometown. And I certainly *never* put myself in danger by tracking down a *real* gangster."

"The world's not the same as when you were a kid."

"It's not *that* different, Matt."

Matt shook his head. "What did Mom say?"

"Your mom wants me to send you to a private military school on the East Coast."

"Great."

"She'll get over it." Matt's dad reclined on the sofa in their living room and flipped on the television with a remote. "What I'm saying, Matt, is that your mother and I are more than a little concerned that your enthusiasm for writing has got you living out the fantasy adventures you're writing about. But life isn't make-believe. It's real."

"I know that," Matt agreed.

"I don't think you do. You're acting like you think the fantasies you write can actually happen. Your mom and I have agreed that you'll be grounded for a month, starting tomorrow."

"What? You can't—a *month*?"

"It's for your own good, Matt," Stan Calahan said. "You need a break. And we're going to ground you from your laptop, too."

"*What!* Okay, yeah, you know, you're right. It's me. I've been acting crazy! But, hey, you don't need to take away my laptop. You just need to ground me to my room. Lock me in my prison."

"Well, we're doing that, too. But we're not changing our minds."

"Dad! You don't understand."

"Then help me. Look, I give up using my cell phone all the time. You said you would try to give up this ... obsession with your laptop. But it has gotten worse."

"It's not an obsession—Dad, it's different."

"Four weeks," Mr. Calahan said. "It's not the end of the world."

"It could be."

Matt's dad turned up the volume on the TV. Matt stood up and stormed out of the room.

"Oh—and Matt?"

Matt stopped, not turning around.

"Don't forget to take out the trash and set the alarm. And one more thing."

Matt waited. "What?"

"I love you."

Matt huffed. "I know."

"And, despite the danger ... well done. On all accounts."

Matt smiled then.

At the end of the driveway, Matt met Isabel by the trash cans. She must have been watching, because as soon as he hit the end of the driveway, she was there, over on his side of the street.

"Hey," Matt said, smiling kindly.

"Hey," she returned.

Matt reached in his jacket pocket and pulled out a CD. "I was hoping I'd see you," he said before he could retract the admission. "Uh, I mean, I brought you a CD."

Isabel accepted the CD.

"Her name's Rebecca St. James," Matt said. "She's a good singer. We normally listen to more guy groups, but she has a cool sound."

After looking at the cover, Isabel's right eyebrow popped up. "You guys like her just because of her sound. Right." She smirked.

Matt shrugged.

"I'm just kidding," Isabel said, smiling.

Matt let out a long breath. "I know. I just got grounded. For a month."

"Ouch. But ... thank you. I mean for helping with the house. Not for getting grounded."

Matt smiled back. "You're welcome. It, uh, was worth it."

"I told you before I didn't need a hero to rescue me. But ... well, I'm glad I know one anyway."

Matt felt color rise to his cheeks. "It's too bad you don't get to keep the gold," he said, changing the subject.

Isabel looked down the street. "Ah, I don't want dirty money anyway."

Matt nodded.

"Besides," she looked back at Matt, her brown eyes swallowing him up, "I've discovered something more rewarding. In Jesus."

"I'm really sorry for not saying something sooner," Matt apologized, still kicking himself. "I'm supposed to be a good example. You know, that's part of the whole 2:52 thing."

"Matt," she said, touching his arm. "You did say something. Every day. *Through* your example."

For the next twenty minutes, Matt and Isabel stood outside and froze and talked—but mostly talked—about the chase, about the race, and about what it meant to be a Christian. Matt felt like he could stand there all night. For he knew that when he went back inside, his life would stop cold for a month.

That is, if Sam ... if Wordtronix ... if this crazy new world of thirteen would let it.

Epilogue

"What do you mean you're not fit enough?" Matt asked Hulk.

"I mean, Calhan, dat I need ta be in tip-top shape for wrestlin'. Rumor is Coach wants ta start a team."

"So . . . ," Matt pressed, closing his locker.

"Well, remember how ya helped me in English a while back?"

Matt squeezed the bridge of his nose with his forefinger and his thumb. "How could I forget?" He was still recovering from Hulk's lame haiku. Why was he forever writing poetry about bodily functions?

"Well," the big lug continued, "yer skinny. I figure ya can help me lose weight, too."

"You want me to put you on a diet?"

"Don't gimme attitude, Calhan. Ya owe me one."

Matt rolled his eyes. "I'm grounded. I can't even leave my house."

Hulk threw a meaty fist in front of Matt's face. "Den find a way to get outta it, or yer gonna find out what it means ta be grounded!"

Matt sighed. Without his laptop, this would be some challenge. Still, better *that* than a crushed face.

"I'll see what I can do."

To be continued . . .

How to Use the Roman Road

A Cool and Deep Way to Lead Your Friends to Jesus!

by Lamar Whitmore

(as stolen from Pastor Ruhlen, who probably stole it from an anonymous place)

Okay, here are five Scriptures you can use when leading your friends to Jesus.

Underneath each one I put what it means so you can share that with your friends.

Romans 3:23: "For all have sinned and fall short of the glory of God."

We've all done stuff that's wrong. Because of that, we don't deserve to go to heaven.

Romans 5:8: "But God demonstrates his own love for us in this: While we were still sinners, Christ died for us."

God loves us a ton. Because He knew we didn't deserve to go to heaven, He sent His Son, Jesus, to earth. Jesus never did anything wrong, but he was killed anyway. We were the ones who deserved death, but when Jesus died and rose again, He took our place—so we wouldn't have to die.

Romans 6:23: "For the wages of sin is death, but the gift of God is eternal life in Christ Jesus our Lord."

Yes, doing wrong leads to death, but God's gift to us is Jesus. And if we make Him the ruler of our lives, we can live forever with Him in heaven.

Romans 10:9–10: "If you confess with your mouth, 'Jesus is Lord,' and believe in your heart that God raised him from the dead, you will be saved. For it is with your heart that you believe and are justified, and it is with your mouth that you confess and are saved."

To make Jesus your Lord, all you have to do is say that you believe He is Lord, and then believe in your heart that He died and rose again for you.

Romans 10:13: "Everyone who calls on the name of the Lord will be saved."

Count on it: God will hear your prayer—and you will be saved!

About the Author

For nearly ten years, Christopher P. N. Maselli has been sharing God's Word with kids through stories. He is the author of multiple award-winning projects including an international children's magazine, a middle-grade adventure novel series, videos, and more.

Chris lives in Fort Worth, Texas, with his wife, Gena, and their feline twins, Zoë and Zuzu. He is actively involved in his church's *KIDS Church* program, and his hobbies include inline skating, collecting *It's a Wonderful Life* movie memorabilia, and "way too much" computing.

What is  SOUL GEAR ?

Based on Luke 2:52:
"And Jesus grew in wisdom and stature,
and in favor with God and men (NIV)."

2:52 is designed just for boys 8-12! This verse is one of
the only verses in the Bible that provides a glimpse of
Jesus as a young boy. Who doesn't wonder what Jesus
was like as a kid?

Become smarter, stronger, deeper, and cooler as you
develop into a young man of God with 2:52 Soul Gear™!

The 2:52 Soul Gear™ takes a closer look by focusing on the
four major areas of development highlighted in Luke 2:52:

"Wisdom" = mental/emotional = **Smarter**

"Stature" = physical = **Stronger**

"Favor with God" = spiritual = **Deeper**

"Favor with man" = social = **Cooler**

Zonder**kidz**.

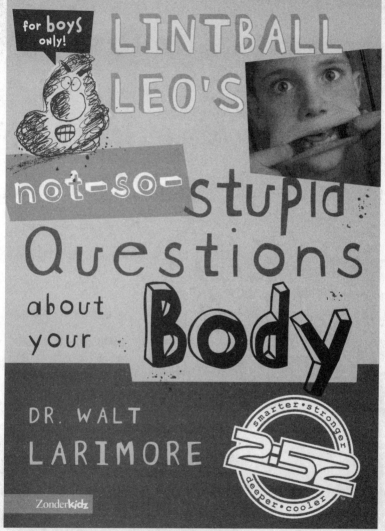

Everything a boy should know, but won't ask!

for boys only!

LINTBALL LEO'S not-so- stupid Questions about your Body

DR. WALT LARIMORE

2:52 · smarter · stronger · deeper · cooler

Zonderkidz

with John RIDDLE Illustrations by Mike Phillips

Softcover 0-310-70545-2

Zonderkidz

"That long?" asked Steve.

"Ah, it goes fast. Especially when you start thinking about *girls*."

Steve blushed bright red.

"Puberty can be a pretty confusing time," Leo said. "But it helps if you remember it's all part of growing up. God made your body and this is the way he wants it to work—so don't sweat it."

"What if I don't *want* to go through puberty?" asks Steve.

"Unfortunately, that's not an option," Leo sighed. "When the time is right for you, it will just happen.

Then, you'll become a man. That's the good news."

"How old are you?" Steve tried to get a better look at Leo. Are you older than dirt?"

"Very funny, Steve. Let me give you some advice. I've been here and there over the years, and I've seen the good, the bad, and the ugly."

"*Now* you're talking about girls." Steve joked.

"Hey, another funny one. No, I'm not talking about girls. I'm talking about boys and how puberty affects them."

Steve looked worried. "Will this puberty thing hurt? I mean should I wear a helmet?"

With that Lintball Leo rolled up into a ball and

Get Smarter

Growing up isn't easy to do. It would be less complicated if there were a training manual telling you what to expect throughout puberty. But we don't have a manual, and even if we did, everybody grows at a different pace and in a different way. Get smart by finding an older male you can talk to. The best person would be your dad. If he's not available, consider a youth pastor or counselor at your school. Ask very specific questions about growing up. Listen carefully to the answers. Then ask God to help you.

2:52 Soul Gear™ Non-fiction books—
ACTION & ADVENTURE with comic appeal—
straight from the pages of the Bible!

Bible Heroes & Bad Guys
Written by Rick Osborne
Learn about true heroes—and bad guys— in action,
pulled straight from the pages of the Bible
Softcover 0-310-70322-0

Bible Wars & Weapons
Written by Rick Osborne
Experience the thrill and intensity of battle
from the frontlines during Bible times!
Softcover 0-310-70323-9

Bible Fortresses, Temples, & Tombs
Written by Rick Osborne
Uncover hidden mysteries of some of the Bibles well-known—
and not so well known—ancient cities. Get the facts on it all.
Softcover 0-310-70483-9

Weird & Gross Bible Stuff
Written by Rick Osborne
For boys with an appetite for learning about
weird—even grotesque—facts in the Bible.
Softcover 0-310-70484-7

Amazing & Unexplainable Things in the Bible
Written by Rick Osborne & Ed Strauss
Discover some of the most astonishing and miraculous things
you'll ever learn about—straight from the Bible.
Softcover 0-310-70653-X

Coming February 2004!

Creepy Creatures & Bizarre Beasts from the Bible
Written by Rick Osborne
Learn about amazing creatures of the Bible as you discover
the awesome, all-powerful nature of God.
Softcover 0-310-70654-8

Coming February 2004!

Available now at your local bookstore!

Zonder**kidz**.

The 2:52 Boys Bible–
the "ultimate *man*ual" for boys!

The 2:52 Boys Bible, NIV
General Editor Rick Osborne

From the metal-looking cover to the cool features inside, *The 2:52 Boys Bible, NIV* is filled with tons of fun and interesting facts–yup, even gross ones, too!–that only a boy could appreciate. Based on Luke 2:52: "And Jesus grew in wisdom and stature, and in favor with God and men," this Bible will help boys ages 8-12 become more like Jesus mentally, physically, spiritually, and socially–Smarter, Stronger, Deeper, and Cooler!

Hardcover 0-310-70320-4
Softcover 0-310-70552-5

Zonder**kidz**.

We want to hear from you. Please send your comments about this book to us in care of zreview@zondervan.com. Thank you.

Zonder**kidz**®

Grand Rapids, MI 49530
www.zonderkidz.com